NANCY WARREN

HERRINGBONES AND HEXES

VAMPIRE KNITTING CLUB
BOOK TWELVE

Herringbones and Hexes, Vampire Knitting Club Book 12, Copyright © 2021 by
Nancy Warren

Cover Design by Lou Harper of Cover Affairs

ISBN: ebook 978-1-928145-97-4

ISBN: print 978-1-928145-96-7

Ambleside Publishing

INTRODUCTION

What the hex is going on?

Life at Cardinal Woolsey's knitting and yarn shop is about as smooth as shop owner Lucy's knitting. In other words, lumpy, tangled and prone to disaster. Much like her spell-casting. But things get worse when her cousin and shop assistant Violet shows alarming symptoms of a hex. Who would do such a thing? Was it the guy from Witch Date she blew off? Or is Lucy the real target?

Meanwhile, Lucy's dating a much older man. Like five hundred years older. The gorgeous vampire Rafe wants to marry her, but there's more keeping them apart than an age gap. Can they make a May-medieval marriage work? Or will they say goodbye forever?

When someone dies, either the hex is to blame or there's a murderer on the loose in Oxford.

Don't miss the fun in this 12th novel in the best-selling Vampire Knitting Club series from a USA Today Bestselling author. There's no gore, sex or swearing, just romance, humor—

and murder. Come join the Vampire Knitting Club for the fun of it. Knitting skills not required.

"Reading this series is like visiting with beloved friends!"

HERRINGBONES AND HEXES

CHAPTER 1

*T*he trouble with working in a knitting store is that I get to see all the gorgeous patterns as they come in, the glossy magazines that lure me in with the promise that I, too, could buy a few skeins of wool, a pattern and some needles and presto, bingo, end up walking around in a designer knit sweater.

The reality is so much different. I'm trying to get better at knitting. I really am. I've figured out a few of the basics, don't drop so many stitches anymore, and I've even finished a handful of garments. But I tend to fall for the more intricate designs that are, as my friends back in the States would say, way above my pay grade.

Yes, I should knit straight scarves and simple hats. Perhaps one of the simpler tea cozy patterns. But I'm an optimist at heart, and when my eye is drawn to the more complex patterns, my positive-thinking brain asks, how hard could it be?

This particular morning, I was looking at a magazine featuring a herringbone rug. Now, I'm the first to admit that I never knew there was such a stitch as the herringbone until this magazine arrived.

I was lost in wonder when my cousin Violet looked over my

shoulder. "That's pretty. It would look nice beside your bed, Lucy."

"It would." And even the thought that Vi considered me capable of making the rug made me warm to her.

"I'm sure your gran or one of the other vampire knitters could whip that up for you in no time," she added, immediately bursting my bubble.

"No. I want to make it myself."

She flipped her long, black hair over her shoulder. "Are we running before we can walk? Or perhaps in your case, toddling before we can walk? Crawling before we can toddle?"

Before we got to me swishing around in the womb, I held up a hand.

"Probably. But I love how knitting's all about connection. A bit like being a witch." And, yes, I could probably use magic to ease my knitting woes, but what was the point of that? I might as well just let the vampires do all my knitting for me. I wanted to learn. No. That wasn't true. I wanted to be an accomplished knitter. Even being handy with a crochet hook would improve my confidence. Instead, I ran a knitting shop where I was daily reminded of my shortcomings.

When I'd hired my cousin Violet as my shop assistant, I'd wondered if I was doing the right thing. She was also a witch, and it rankled with her that I'd won the struggle for our family grimoire. I'd been as surprised as she was, but witchy power's a funny thing. More innate than learned, though there was plenty of training involved, as I'd recently discovered.

I hadn't asked for it, but I was learning the hard truth that I and my powers were going to be needed in some coming Witchageddon that Margaret Twigg, the leader of our coven, was predicting. I wasn't sure if she really foresaw dire trouble or was using it to prod me into focusing on my training, but I really was trying to master my powers.

I didn't need to strain those powers unduly to notice that Violet seemed more fidgety than usual. She kept finding things to do in the front window. She was reorganizing and dusting my winter woolens window display, which would have been both remarkable and useful on most days, since Violet wasn't usually the first to pick up the duster or the broom. However, I had just redone the window display yesterday, so there was no point to her activity. All she managed to do was annoy Nyx, who was peacefully sleeping in her usual spot, curled up in a basket of wool in my front window.

After having her nose inadvertently dusted and then suffering the final indignity of having her basket moved while she was still in it, Nyx rose onto all fours, glared at Vi, turned all the way around to glare at me, and then jumped down and stalked to the door that separated Cardinal Woolsey's Knitting Shop from the stairway that led to my flat upstairs. She meowed insistently until I walked over and opened the door for her, whereupon she scampered upstairs, no doubt so she could enjoy the rest of her nap in peace.

I was watching Violet, wondering if I was witnessing an incipient nervous breakdown, when she jumped back and put her hand to her chest. "Maybe that's him. Is it him?"

I followed her gaze out the front window and saw a skinny young guy with a lot of tattoos and shoulder-length brown hair. He had a backpack slung over his shoulders. To me, he looked like a typical student in Oxford, but the way Violet was gazing at him anxiously, I suspected she knew him. He turned, and she took another step back away from the window, and then while I watched, a woman about his own age ran up and joined him. They stopped for a kiss and then continued on their way.

"Not him, then," Violet said, and I wasn't certain whether she was sorry or glad.

"Not him what?"

She shook her head as though she'd just come out of a swimming pool. "Sorry. I have a date. I thought that might be him."

"You have a date?" I was quite surprised, since Violet had sworn off men. In fairness, she'd done it more than once, and with pretty good reason. Violet had the worst luck in romance of anyone I'd ever known. Well, not Romeo and Juliet dramatic, not Heloise and Abelard difficult, or Hero and Leander tragic. But in terms of contemporary women—and witches—I knew, Cupid didn't smile on my cousin Violet. So to find out that she was dating again was interesting news.

I was obviously staring at her, so she said, "It's not a big deal, Lucy. I met him on Witch Date."

"Witch Date?" I wasn't even sure how you spelled the service. Was it which, as in which guy should I choose? Or was it witch, as in witches dating witches? That seemed like it was narrowing the dating pool a whole lot. I knew plenty of male witches and was very fond of some of them, but I didn't know any I'd want to date. And with Violet's track record, I wasn't sure that splashing around in the dating witch pool was the best idea.

She put a hand on her hip. "Witch Date is an internet dating site for magical creatures like us."

"I've never heard of it."

She rolled her gaze at me. "It's on the dark net, obviously."

"Oh, obviously." Like I spent so much time on the dark net. In fact, I wasn't even sure how to find it. I suspected she'd be better off if she didn't dip her toes in there either.

In the interests of harmony in the workplace, I didn't share my sense of dread at the new dating adventure. I merely said, "So you have a date with a witch?"

"Yes."

"Have you had other dates with witches?" I couldn't imagine the dating pool was very large here in Oxfordshire. I suspected she'd go through all the single witches seeking other single witches pretty quickly.

"No. This is my first. It's why I'm so nervous."

"Why do you think he'll come here?" It seemed like a reasonable question. This wasn't her house; this was her place of business. And while witches tended to have different powers, clairvoyance wasn't particularly common.

"Because I told him to meet me here."

The hairs rose up on the back of my neck. "You asked a witch to come to my knitting shop to pick you up for a date."

"Well, obviously, I didn't want some stranger with magical powers coming to my house."

"Right. Only to my shop. Because we both know how well that's gone in the past."

I laid the sarcasm on, but honestly, it seemed like any time we had a supernatural creature in the store, bad things happened. And that was leaving out the knitting circle of undead crafters who met late at night in my back room, many of them coming up from the subterranean living complex beneath my shop.

I didn't think it was a good idea to have a witch wandering around up here. Especially not one who hung around on the dark net. All witches weren't good ones, and not all witches were accepting of vampires.

Still, she was nervous enough already. I didn't want to upset her. Maybe he'd turn out to be a great guy.

"Well, if you're going to stand at the window anyway, take some window cleaner and a cloth and polish up the glass." I hadn't had a chance to do that yet.

Even though she was my employee, Violet rarely did what I asked her to, and for a second I thought she'd refuse. Then with a huff, she said, "Fine," and grabbed the cloth I used for doing windows and the spray cleaner.

She climbed right into the front window and was busily cleaning the panes when the door opened. I looked up, assuming it was her date, but to my surprise it was William Thresher, Rafe Crosyer's butler and estate manager. Since Rafe was a vampire, William had very little opportunity to use his absolutely incredible cooking skills, plus he really needed to get out more and mix with mortals, so he'd started up a catering company that was doing well. He was very selective about what clients he took on and which events he agreed to cater, but he'd built a nice business in a short time. I'd helped him a time or two as a waitress, but Violet worked with him regularly.

William was a pleasant-looking man in his mid-thirties. You wouldn't call him handsome, but you wouldn't call him not, either. He wasn't tall or short; he was medium. His build wasn't skinny or large. It was somewhere in the middle. In fact, William was about as average as they come until you got to know him.

William Thresher was the latest in a long line of mortals who had served Rafe. His many times great-grandfather had saved Rafe's life back in the 1500s and sworn complete loyalty to the vampire. Since then, every generation had produced another William Thresher who took his father's place. The trouble was that the current William had no missus. And no progeny. And I could tell that Rafe was getting a little anxious. That was obviously why he had agreed to let William have his little business on the side. No doubt he hoped William would meet some lovely young woman who'd become the future Mrs. Thresher and therefore the mother of the future butler and house manager at Crosyer Manor.

It all seemed very feudal to me, but when I'd asked William whether he didn't feel as though he were some kind of indentured servant, he'd laughed at me. "Lucy, working for Rafe has advantages. He's a very generous employer. Always has been." He didn't say more, but I knew that Rafe, with his hundreds of years of experience of humans, business, and money-making opportunities, was wealthy beyond my wildest imagination. It made perfect sense that he'd steered all the Threshers in the way of a small fortune of their own. Since he provided their lodging, a very nice house on the property, and all their meals and needs, I imagined that nest egg just kept growing and growing, generation after generation. He might look average and unassuming, but I suspected that William was a very wealthy guy.

I didn't think he'd been hanging around on Witch Date, but Violet didn't know that. She hadn't yet seen who'd come in, only heard the door open. She leapt out from the front window and then, when she saw who it was, to my astonishment, she blushed.

She flipped her long, dark hair over her shoulder so that the streak of purple and pink that she liked to dye into the front of her hair floated over her shoulder like a ribbon. "William, what are you doing here?"

I glanced at William and found that his color was slightly heightened too. "Violet. I came to see you, actually."

She dumped the rag and cleaner unceremoniously in Nyx's basket of wools and moved towards William. "You did?"

"I did. I've got another catering job. I wonder if you'd be available?"

Her thrilled expression dropped faster than one of my stitches when I was trying to knit a scarf. Or knit anything for that matter. "Oh. What's the gig?"

"A new client, actually. Somebody very big in finance. It's a select dinner on Saturday night for some of her clients. I need people I can trust."

Well, it wasn't sweet nothings, but Violet was obviously gratified that William respected her in a professional capacity, even if he wasn't scattering rose petals at her feet in a romantic way. I'd harbored suspicions for a while that they were interested in each other, but it was clear neither had acted on their mutual esteem. Perhaps they were both shy or didn't want to ruin a good friendship.

I could tell she wanted to go. Still, she was female. "Saturday? I'm not sure right at the moment. I'll have to go home and check my calendar. I might have a date."

His eyebrows flew up at that. "A date? You're seeing someone then?" Sounded like he was sorry to hear that.

Maybe she'd noticed it too. "Well," she said airily, "I wouldn't exactly call it dating. Early days yet."

"Right. Right." He stood there for a minute more, and I thought he might say something. I wanted to urge him to say something, but I knew better than to nudge these two along with magic. They'd have to figure it out on their own. "Well, let me know when you've checked your calendar."

After he left, Violet threw her head back and sent out a yell of frustration. "Saturday night? He comes in here looking for me to waitress on a Saturday night?"

"Well, he does run a catering company, and you do waitress for him on a regular basis."

She swung around at me as though I'd said something completely inappropriate. "I am a woman, Lucy. A very attractive woman. Doesn't he think I might have something else to do on a Saturday night?"

"I'm sure he does. And maybe this Witch Date guy will turn out to be the one and you'll be completely in love by Saturday night."

She glared at me as though I was being sarcastic, but I really wasn't. Not very. "Right. It could happen." She flipped her hair over her shoulders. "I could definitely be in love by Saturday night."

CHAPTER 2

*N*aturally, between wondering if her date would show up and being annoyed with William for assuming she'd be free on a Saturday evening, Violet forgot all about the windows. It was me who picked up the cleaner and the rag and put them away while she wandered around the shop picking things up and putting them down and not doing anything useful.

Every time the door opened, she'd take a couple of steps forward and scrutinize whoever came in. Three times in a row, it was a customer looking for patterns, wool or, in the last case, directions to the closest public toilet. The fourth time the door opened, I think we both knew it was her date.

He had bleached hair that stuck out in tufts all over his head and wore a black jacket, jeans, and a shirt that had seen better days. A silver pentagram hung around his neck on a strip of black leather.

He looked at me and he looked at Violet and then he raised his eyebrows. "Mistress Moon?"

I glared at Violet. Really? Mistress Moon? I couldn't believe he'd shown up to the date.

There was a slightly too long silence, and I had a sneaking feeling Violet was hoping I'd own up to that terrible pseudonym. I turned and glared until she stepped forward. "Hello. You must be Forest Sprite."

He laughed and held out his hand. "Leo." He looked slightly bashful. "Like the lion."

She shook his hand. "Violet. Like the flower."

"And are you? A shrinking violet?"

Oh, this was going to go well. I'd always thought Violet associated herself more with the color than a woodland bloom. She gave him a tight smile.

"This is a cool place you've got here." He stood for a moment and appeared to be listening. "Interesting vibes. Some weird energy."

"It's the customers," Violet assured him. "You wouldn't believe the people we get in here. Some of them are so old, they're practically dead."

She said it in an airy tone, but I gave her the stink eye anyway.

Leo said, "I noticed there's a tea shop next door. Do you want to go and have a cup?"

Naturally, Violet didn't bother to ask my permission to leave. She said, "Sure. Let me grab my handbag."

"Bye," Leo said, holding the door open for Violet, which at least showed he had manners.

"See you later," Violet said as she breezed out the door.

I glanced at my watch. It was four o'clock. Unless the date went really badly, I wouldn't see her again that day, as we closed the shop at five. She was lucky I was such an easygoing employer. And related by blood.

We weren't that busy, and if Violet could find romance, I thought she'd be a lot happier. She was my cousin, after all, and I was fond of her.

But Witch Date?

~

As I had suspected, when five o'clock came, I was all by myself. I was just finished closing up and about to head upstairs when my cell phone rang. It was Rafe.

Rafe Crosyer was impossible to describe. A vampire who'd walked the earth for five hundred years, he still looked as fresh as the day he'd been turned. Apart from being slightly pale, he looked thirty-five, gorgeous, with a slightly intellectual air that frankly made me weak at the knees.

We had a complicated relationship. He protected me, though he could be old-fashioned to the point of controlling. He was also kind, generous, and he'd saved my life more than once. He was also in love with me.

When Rafe proposed, I'd been thrilled and horrified at the same time. So much of me wanted to marry him. I liked his intelligence, his wit. He was a brilliant knitter, kept our local nest of vampires orderly and safe. He could be overprotective, but I knew it came from deep love.

However, no relationship was perfect, and ours had the pretty much insurmountable issue that I would live, age, and die as a mortal woman while he remained unchangeable, and he'd go on after I was dead. I didn't know who I felt more sorry for in this scenario, him or me. For right now, it was fine. I was approaching thirty. He still looked thirty-five and always would. But what about later?

We hadn't talked about children, but I was pretty sure he couldn't have them. How did I feel about that?

Sure, the option of him turning me into a vampire was out there, but I didn't have a lot of interest in the whole undead thing.

And so I decided I would tell him no. I'd made that decision more than once. Then I'd see him again and somehow the words wouldn't leave my mouth. This had been going on long enough, though. I had to make up my mind. Yes or no.

I leaned toward no when I wasn't with him because I could be clear about all the reasons why it would be difficult. But when I was with him? I just wanted to be with him, and then I'd think, maybe. It seemed to me that he was the one who had the most to lose, and if he was willing to live with me in a way that would be permanent for me and temporary for him, who was I to tell him no? At his age, he must know his own mind.

Also in the plus column, he didn't push me for an answer. I knew he was waiting, and I knew I had to make up my mind. But maybe not right now.

"Lucy. I'm calling on behalf of William, who wants you to taste-test a meal he has in mind to serve at his next catering function. And I want your opinion on something."

"Okay." Rafe rarely needed my opinion on anything. He was an antiquarian book expert, and I ran a knitting shop.

"I've come across a rather curious book. I think you should see it."

"A knitting book?"

"No. An alchemist's book. One I've never seen before. It's very old." When Rafe said very old, he thought in centuries rather than decades.

Rafe didn't sound lonely, but I suspected this curious book was an excuse. Besides, I didn't have anything more interesting upstairs than a frozen lasagna I'd bought at my local Tesco. Whereas William was the catering equivalent of a Michelin-starred restaurant.

"I'll just get changed and feed Nyx and I'll be right over."

And so I ran upstairs, showered and changed my clothes. I

fed Nyx, and as she watched me get ready for my sort of date, I swear she shook her head at me.

"I don't know how many lives you've had, Nyx, but I suspect this isn't your first. What do I do?"

She walked up to me, sat down, looked up at me with her big, green-gold eyes and meowed. No doubt she was giving me great advice, if only I spoke cat.

Sometimes Nyx seemed to put thoughts into my head, but I didn't get anything more than that plaintive meow.

I jumped in my little red car and drove out to Crosyer Manor. The Georgian mansion was a welcoming place with all the lights on. Knowing William was busy doing wonders in the kitchen, I wondered if Rafe would answer the door to me himself. I knocked, preparing to treat him like the butler.

Then the door opened and a blond-haired woman was standing there. She wore a figure-hugging black dress, low-heeled black shoes, and makeup. She smiled when she saw me.

"Lucy."

"Olivia," I answered. "I've never seen you in a dress before." Oh, not my finest moment. "I mean—"

She laughed. "I know exactly what you mean. Whenever you see me, I'm usually knee-deep in dirt and mud, planting or weeding."

It was true. Olivia Thresher was William's sister. Even though the deal was that the eldest son became Rafe's butler and head of his household from generation to generation, it seemed that a lot of the other kids ended up working for him too. I imagined it was a pretty sweet gig. And so Olivia, William's younger sister, was Rafe's gardener. But not tonight.

She opened the door wider and stepped back. "Come in." She shook her head. "I'm not very good at this. It's why I hardly ever take William's place. I'm much better communing with plants and trees and sheep and woodland animals than with people."

"You're doing just fine. And anyway, I don't know why Rafe couldn't open the door himself."

She put her hand over her mouth to stifle a giggle. She had short fingernails and work-hardened hands.

"Rafe is perfectly willing to open the door himself," the man himself said, stepping forward. "But, between them, William and Olivia don't seem to believe I'm capable of the exertion."

Her eyes twinkled, but she said seriously, "We've your position in society to protect. The master of the house does not open his own door."

His aristocratic nose rose slightly at that. "In this century, I believe they do."

"William would be miserable if someone wasn't here to serve you," she said as she took my coat.

"Lucy," he said, giving me the smile that he never gave to anyone else. "You look very nice."

Suddenly I felt flustered. I had dressed with care. I wore a blue dress that Dr. Christopher Weaver had knitted for me. I had an even nicer one that Sylvia had knitted for me, but since I was currently annoyed with Sylvia, I refused to wear any of her clothes.

She'd been trying to be nice to me in our last few vampire knitting club meetings, but I remained cool. When someone nearly gets you killed, it takes a while to get over.

Though I didn't say it, Rafe also looked really good. He wore a dark green, cashmere pullover so fine the wool must have had silk in it, black trousers and shiny black loafers. His hair was raven's wing black. His eyes could be almost glacial, but not when he was looking at me.

He held up his hand, and I took it. I'd learned to like the slightly cool touch.

14

"I thought we'd look at the book first, and by then William should be ready for you."

"Yes, that's fine with me."

"Bring drinks into the library, will you, Olivia?"

"Right away."

"Honestly, you didn't need to bring the gardener in to act like your butler."

"They have their way of doing things, and I have learned to respect that. Lucy, what your generation fails to understand, as you try to pretend everyone is equal and fail so spectacularly, is that a good butler takes his position seriously and has pride in his work. For me to open my own door would be like taking my glove and striking William on the cheek."

"Okay, I could see that, except that William and his sister are from this generation."

"They've been trained to consider it their duty to look after me. Their father trained them as his father trained him and so on."

I was beginning to understand now. "And you feel it's your duty to look after them."

"I do."

"What are you going to do if William doesn't find someone to marry and make some new William Threshers?"

He looked down his nose at me. "In five hundred years, it's never happened. If it does now, I'll cope."

I was genuinely curious. "Would you take Olivia's firstborn son if William didn't have any kids?"

"Since William is only thirty-seven years old and in the prime of life, I hardly think we need to consider such eventualities."

Which is when I knew he had thought of it, and most likely that was the solution he had in mind too. Except that Olivia was no closer to wedded bliss and parenthood than her brother.

He looked out the window and then back at me. "I appreciate that you're American and from a country that prizes freedom above all. If me having servants makes you uncomfortable, you could reorder this house as you wish."

My heart jumped up and down behind my ribcage. Here he was referring to his as yet unanswered marriage proposal, as though that would be a reason I would refuse to marry him.

"Rafe," I said. And then I got tongue-tied and stuck. "If William and Olivia want to work here, then of course they should. If I married you, I wouldn't want to change that."

His smile was bittersweet. "If. We're still at if, are we?"

I felt my cheeks heating. "I don't know what to say. I want to give you an answer. I know I need to. But I don't know what to do."

He walked over and sat beside me. He lifted my chin with one long finger and leaned forward and kissed me lightly. "And when you do, you'll tell me."

Before I could verbalize one of the many thoughts that were tumbling around in my head and heart, he said, "Come. Have a look at this."

CHAPTER 3

*I*t was a relief not to continue the conversation, so I followed eagerly to his desk.

The book he showed me appeared to be a grimoire. There was nothing particularly astonishing in this. We had a fairly sizable coven of witches in our area. Most of us had a grimoire, some of them, like mine, very old. And Rafe had seen plenty of them in his time. I wasn't sure what had caught his notice.

He donned cotton gloves to handle the volume on his desk and handed me a pair. The book wasn't remarkable on the outside—simple leather bindings, some markings too faded to make out—but when he opened the cover, the pages were amazing, with brightly colored drawings.

"This must be a fake," I said, "or it would be badly faded."

"That's what's so curious. It's not. All my tests show the paper, the ink, and cover all consistent with the 1500s."

"Is that Latin?" The writing was clear, too, but in a language I couldn't read.

"Yes."

We both looked at the page. He turned it, and another, just

as colorful, appeared. "It's like it was written yesterday. Do you think it's a spell?"

"Most likely."

"Where did it come from?"

"New Zealand. Taken there from France, I believe. I purchased it from a collector who now wants me to value and authenticate their entire collection."

"It's absolutely fascinating." I felt an urge to touch. I slipped on the gloves and moved closer. Before I even touched the pages, I felt the magic. "Oh, yes," I found myself whispering. "There's a spell on this book." I was dazzled by the drawings.

"Alchemy was often aligned with magic."

I smiled. "Someone trying to turn base metal into gold?"

"Or looking for the secret to endless youth."

I glanced at him sharply. "But you found that."

"Yes. And not through potions and strange incantations."

"It's wonderful. What do you plan to do with it?" I asked.

"I'll translate it first, then try to work out whose work it is."

"What about the spell?"

"Oh, I'll leave the magic undisturbed. It's kept this volume in pristine condition all this time. If you can work out how the spell was done, there are a few precious volumes I'd be pleased to protect in a similar fashion."

Olivia arrived then, looking flustered. "William says could you come to the table? He's worried the first course won't keep."

Before answering, he looked at me. "Is that all right with you, Lucy?"

I was always ready to eat William's creations, so I nodded, hopefully not too eagerly.

She ran on ahead, and we took a more leisurely stroll to the dining room. When Olivia was out of earshot, I said, "She's obviously more comfortable outside with the plants."

"It's good for her to become accustomed to working inside the house as well. We haven't the staff we once did."

"Well, she's getting some practice tonight."

Rafe said, "And Olivia will look after me again on Saturday night when William caters a dinner for his financial advisor."

In my shop, William had described the person who was hosting that dinner as a big shot in finance. He hadn't mentioned the client was also William's personal advisor. I looked at Rafe. "So William's financial advisor's a pretty big deal, I understand."

The vampire looked at me in surprise. "Why? Are you in need of a financial advisor?"

"Come on, Rafe. I'm trying to figure out how rich William really is."

"How vulgar of you."

I rolled my eyes. "He's my friend. I'm curious. Is he as rich as you?"

He looked down his long nose at me. "Lucy."

I don't know why I enjoyed teasing him so much. "Okay, but is he wealthy?"

"How does one define wealthy? There are so many levels of monetary wealth."

If I kept rolling my eyeballs around in my head, I was worried I would do myself damage, so I restrained myself with difficulty. "Is he a millionaire? Multi-millionaire? Billionaire? I don't know what comes after billionaire, gazillionaire?"

"This is a very improper discussion. William is quite well-to-do. I've made sure of it."

"You're not going to tell me anything, are you?"

"Certainly not. I fail to see why you should want to know William's affairs."

Even though I was curious, I respected that Rafe wasn't a

blabbermouth. "Aren't you afraid he'll get so rich that he won't need you anymore? That he won't want to stay in your service?"

"No. I'm not. As I believe I've told you, Lucy, William and Olivia are under no compulsion to remain with me. They choose to do so."

"I think if I was a multimillionaire—" I shot a glance up at him from under my lashes, but he refused to be drawn. "Or a billionaire...?" Still nothing. Not by the flicker of an eyelash did he give me even a hint of William's wealth. "I'd quit my job and enjoy a life of leisure."

"Ah, would you, though?"

As we passed through the drawing room, he went to the fireplace, where a fire crackled in the hearth. He probably didn't even think about it. There were always fires in his fireplace in the winter, like magic. Not magic, though. Human servants made all this happen. He looked down into the jumping flames.

"I've had a great deal of time to consider this problem. Look at me. I can satisfy your nosy curiosity about myself. You've never asked, but if you're looking for categories, I'm a very quiet billionaire. You won't find me on any list. I keep an extremely low profile, and I pay people a great deal of money to keep it that way."

A billionaire? I would have said I didn't know any billionaires if I'd ever been asked. Turned out I was wrong. So wrong.

"I certainly don't need to work. However, it's my work that gives my time purpose. Like that book we were just studying, for instance. It's a puzzle. Where has it come from? Why did I feel compelled to buy it? Why did I feel drawn to show it to you?

"I have been privileged to study and evaluate everything from Dead Sea Scrolls to first editions of *Harry Potter*." He cast a glance at me. "You'd be amazed at the prices people will pay for that which is considered both rare and desirable. And the things that people fake."

I knew he was serious and trying to explain what his life was like, but I'm sorry, the word billionaire was rolling around in my head like a loose dime in a washing machine.

Billionaire?

Obviously, I could tell from the way he lived, his beautiful manor house and bits of conversation I'd overheard that he was a man of means. I'd imagined there were millions. Millions I could cope with.

But billions?

He was looking at me, waiting for me to respond. Money. Right. And the things people would do for it. Fake books and manuscripts at auction. I had a billion things to think about when I was alone, but now I tried to focus and respond in a sensible way to his assertion that retirement wasn't very exciting.

There were plenty of days I'd have been willing to give retirement a try, even at my young age. "It's different, though, being mortal. Let's say we're lucky and we make it to eighty or ninety years old. By the time you've worked for forty years or so, how bad would it be to get the other twenty off?"

"You must ask William and Olivia. They're both in a position where they could choose idleness over work, and in both cases, they choose work." The way he said idleness made it clear what he thought of retirement. Or at least early retirement.

"So your system is that the William Thresher of the day fathers the William Thresher of tomorrow, and when that young man reaches a certain age, the dad gets to retire."

"It's a fluid proposition but essentially, yes."

"I guess it's not that different from my grandmother leaving me her wool shop after she passed." But did I really want to have a daughter just so I could pass on my business to her? What if she turned out to be a worse knitter than I was? If that was even possible.

Maybe she'd want to be a ballerina or a scientist, something other than a shopkeeper in Oxford. Still, I could see that my little world was very different from Rafe's.

"And William obviously has a side business that he loves."

"He does."

"Violet's going to be working for him on Saturday. Maybe she'll meet a rich guy. We both know she'll be working with one."

He held up an admonishing finger. "Lucy. Even though I've been careful not to answer your questions, I would still appreciate your discretion, especially where your cousin Violet is concerned. And most especially where Violet and William are concerned. We live peaceably here because we keep such a low profile."

How did he do it? He couldn't have seen William and Violet together very often and yet he'd nosed out their possible infatuation.

I felt awful then. "You know I'd never tell anyone. Violet's my cousin but maybe not the most discreet woman in Oxford. I'll keep my mouth shut. I have a vested interest in you and William being safe too, you know."

His eyes glinted when he smiled. "I'm very glad to hear it."

I wanted to ask whether he suspected a fondness between Vi and William. It seemed as though he did, but I decided to keep my suspicions to myself. First, because that's all I had, a suspicion that they liked each other. If Violet was hanging out on Witch Date, then they obviously hadn't taken the attraction anywhere. I kind of hoped it fizzled out. I wasn't sure Violet was the right wife for William, and I was almost positive Rafe would hate the idea of Violet and William as a couple. Much better for me to let things take their course. Maybe Forest Sprite had already swept Mistress Moon off her feet.

"And now, shall we go in to dinner and see what William has prepared for you?"

"Can't wait. I'm starving."

William never let me down. Tonight's dinner was as much theater as food. Each course was presented in such an unusual way that I wanted to hang the plates on the walls, as they seemed too pretty to eat.

From tiny, perfect pastry parcels of an indescribably delicious duck filling, served on tiny bare tree branches, to a salad of local greens to lamb chops with a fig glaze and swirls of green mousse and tiny, perfect vegetables, I was kept in rapture.

Rafe poured the wines, a different one for each course. He even tasted my meal, though he seemed to take more pleasure in watching me eat and hearing my rave reviews.

"Olivia, this is fabulous," I said when she came to clear away my embarrassingly empty plate. "I've never tasted a meal so flavorful."

Even though she hadn't cooked it, I felt like I should give her the compliment by proxy and hope that she remembered to pass it on to William. But to my great delight, I'd managed to compliment her without even realizing it. She smiled at me, looking happier than she had since I'd stepped into the manor house this evening.

"Thank you, Lucy. I grew all those vegetables myself. They're all from the estate."

I smiled at her. "So you're William's secret weapon. As he always tells me, a great chef starts with great ingredients."

She laughed. "I'm sure he's never said any such thing. William is convinced his talent is a kind of magic."

"Well, I know from magic, and ingredients matter."

"Do you have room for dessert?"

The way she said it, I knew dessert was going to be something I would not be able to turn down. Still, I didn't want to be too easy. "Depends what it is."

"Pear tart served with stem ginger ice cream."

"And a very nice Madeira to go with it," Rafe added.

"The pears came from our trees. I tasted some myself earlier. It really is quite delicious."

"Sold."

And so I ended my work day with a meal that would have costs hundreds of pounds in a top London restaurant.

When William came out to ask my opinion on each course, I was able to tell him that I'd enjoyed every perfect bite.

"No criticism at all?"

"Maybe you could make the portions bigger."

CHAPTER 4

*I*t was midmorning the next day, and I'd decided to take the morning off so I could get ahead on my knitting. We weren't very busy in the shop, and if I was there, I'd be doing computer work, which I could just as well do here at Rafe's manor house without having Violet sneak off for extra breaks because she knew I was on the premises.

Rafe was in his office translating the alchemy book, and I was in the living room, where a cozy fire popped and sighed as though commiserating with me as I struggled to make sense of the herringbone rug pattern. It shouldn't be this difficult. I was college-educated, surrounded by wonderful knitters. But I was trying to learn a new stitch that involved knitting two together and dropping one, purling two together and dropping one, which had sounded so much easier when I read it and wasn't so easy when I tried to do it. On top of that, I was trying to make sense of the rug pattern. As I looked down at the instructions, I began to feel the way I used to in an algebra exam when all I saw were marks on a paper that didn't make any sense.

When William walked in, I'd never been so glad to see

anyone in my life. "Tell me you know how to knit," I said the minute I saw him.

He shook his head. "Sorry." When he looked at the mess in my lap, he must have realized I didn't know either. He looked almost embarrassed. "Lucy, could I get your help with something in the kitchen?"

William was calm and unflappable and knew his work better than anyone. What could he possibly need me for? Still, I didn't care if he wanted me to scrub out the fridge. It was better than trying to figure out this mess I'd made. I got to my feet, happily abandoning my knitting. "Sure. What's up?"

"I'm meeting with the people who hired me for Saturday's dinner. They're very particular. They've come around to go over the menu, and I thought it might help if I told them that I'd already cooked everything for you and you were satisfied."

"Satisfied? Try died and gone to heaven."

"I offered to cook the whole thing again for them, but they don't have time."

They already sounded like difficult clients to me. "Are you sure it's worth your time? Why don't you blow them off? Tell them to call Gordon Ramsay. I'm sure he'll change his menu around because they say so."

He smiled at my brutal suggestion. "I might consider it, but one of them is my personal financial advisor." He made a funny face. "I don't want to get on the wrong side of the woman who handles my money."

I laughed. "Definitely not. One bad meal and your net worth could drop by ten percent."

I was joking, but he looked absolutely horrified at the suggestion. If I lost ten percent of my net worth, I wouldn't be thrilled, but truth was it wouldn't be that much money. William's position was obviously different.

I followed him into the big kitchen that was his domain. He

could have held a meeting in his own house on the property or even Rafe's fancy dining room, but I imagined he'd chosen this kitchen because it was so professional. It was clear that a serious chef worked here.

He had the menu laid out on the marble work surface, a computer open, and two people stood gazing at the menu pages. One of them had a Montblanc pen in her hand, and it looked like she was making changes.

William was an artist. When he put together a meal, it was complete. I got the feeling in my chest like she'd taken a paintbrush to a Picasso and was trying to improve it. No wonder William looked so uncharacteristically shaken up.

He brought me in and said, "I'd like to introduce you to Lucy Swift. I cooked the entire meal for Lucy. She's got a very good palate, so I often test menus on her." What a diplomatic way to say I loved to eat.

The two people looked up from their low-voiced conversation. The woman holding the Montblanc pen was introduced as Jemima Taft. She held out a hand to shake mine. A tennis bracelet glinted with diamonds, and her fingers were perfectly manicured. "Pleasure to meet you," she said in one of those posh, well-bred voices. She was an attractive woman about my age with blond, artfully streaked hair so silky and straight that it must have cost a fortune. Everything about her was sleek and expensive. Nobody got that accent in England going to a regular school. Hers spoke of ponies and boarding school and privilege. Her clothing was understated, but I recognized the cashmere in her sweater and the discreet designer logo on her handbag.

The man beside her was Nico Marino. He had wavy, black hair combed back off his face, a thin face with a sharp nose and deep-set, very dark eyes.

Where she seemed calm and controlled, he was all energy

barely contained. He looked like he should be in a Lamborghini racing down the Amalfi Coast.

"It's very important that everything be perfect," Jemima said. I got the feeling it wasn't the first time.

William was too nice for this. He didn't need to do these dinners and catered events. He did it for the love of cooking and making people happy through perfect combinations of flavors offered in a convivial setting. This woman might handle his finances, but she sure didn't know how to handle him.

I said, "William cooked me that whole meal. I can't even tell you how fabulous it was." I smiled at him. "One of the best things about being a frequent visitor to Crosyer Manor is that I get to be William's guinea pig."

She glanced at Nico and then back at me. "I wish we had time to sample everything. But unfortunately we don't." She tapped the printed menu with her pen. "I'm worried about the combination of pear and ginger. You didn't find it too acidic?"

I leaned my elbows on the cool surface of the kitchen island. "William isn't just technically proficient. He's an artist. Your guests are going to think they've died and gone to heaven."

She tapped the paper again. "I was wondering about swapping this salad out for something more grand. Bit plebian, isn't it, a salad?"

I vehemently shook my head. "William could explain it better than I, but his flavors work almost like a symphony. If you change one movement for another, the sound will be all wrong. Unless you have guests with food allergies, leave it to William."

She glanced at her companion again, but he looked like he had a lot of places he should be like five minutes ago. "It will be fine. Stop worrying."

She put away her pen. "Yes. All right then."

Nico turned to William with a piercing stare. "We are trusting you. This is a very important dinner."

It was almost a threat underneath the words "We are trusting you." As in, if you let us down, there will be consequences.

There was a moment. Kind of a tense one. And then Jemima laughed, a silvery laugh that she probably learned in boarding school along with how to hire servants. "We're very grateful, William. We're so looking forward to your food. We've heard so much about it."

And then they finalized the arrangements and left.

I turned to William, who looked slightly stunned by the encounter. "Are you sure about this?"

"You don't think I can satisfy them?" Now he looked like he was losing his confidence.

I shook my head. "Not at all. Your food is magnificent. I just wondered if you wanted to waste it on people who might not appreciate it."

He suddenly smiled. When William smiled, he didn't look so ordinary. His smile was his best feature and very charming. "I shall take it as a challenge. I'm bound and determined there won't be a single complaint."

"I can almost guarantee there will be poems and songs of praise written in your honor after they finish eating."

He gave me a one-armed hug. "There's a reason I brought you in, Lucy. Thank you. They simply needed someone to confirm that their guests would be happy."

"From how snooty they seemed, I'm surprised they didn't hire a big celebrity chef." I'd joked about hiring Gordon Ramsay, but now I wondered if they weren't the types to equate fame with quality.

"It's about discretion, you see. People at her dinner will be very high net worth individuals. They like to keep their business very private."

That made sense. I knew how secretive Rafe was. And I suspected there were more truly wealthy people flying below the radar than there were talked about in the business pages. I knew if I was that rich, I wouldn't want everyone to know either.

"What's Nico's story?"

"I have no idea. He's one of Jemima's clients. She's putting on the dinner to introduce him to other wealthy people who might be useful to him. I believe he's got some business or investment venture in mind. But, as I said, it's very hush-hush."

"I wish I was so rich I'd get invited to that dinner," I said wistfully. They'd left the printout on the kitchen island, and I was staring at it.

"Never knew you were so concerned with wealth."

I glanced up. "Oh, I'm not. I want to eat that meal again."

He chuckled. "I'll make sure to cook extras."

Instantly, I felt happier. "Do. I will expect a very large doggie bag."

CHAPTER 5

"How was the fancy dinner on Saturday night?" I asked Violet when she came in for work Monday morning. I was glad she'd been serving at William's dinner, as she was always up for a good gossip.

"Fine," she snapped. So not what I was hoping for.

She didn't look like a woman who'd had a wonderful break since I'd last seen her Saturday afternoon.

I thought part of it might be that Leo the witch hadn't asked her out for Saturday night, so she'd ended up being free to serve at William's dinner.

"I've never heard from Leo. Not that I wanted to. But it's the principle of the thing. And even though he was as interesting as a wet weekend, I'm not. I'm a wonderful woman. He'd be lucky to get a second date with me. And then he didn't even ask."

I tried to think of something positive to say. "Probably he could sense that you weren't that interested in him, so he wanted to save his pride."

She flipped her hair off her shoulder. "I suppose so." She got very dramatic. "So there I was, Saturday night, with nothing better to do than to scurry along to waitress for William—"

"Come on, you know how much William relies on you. He especially came into the shop to ask you because he had to have servers he could trust."

"I suppose."

"How was the food?"

"Yeah, good. Jemima Taft, who put on the dinner, made sure I got a nice tip. Said the meal was excellent."

"Good. And did she compliment him on the wines?" I recalled whenever I'd helped William how the expensive wines tended to flow at his exclusive, catered dinners.

To my surprise, Violet said, "No. She took me aside at the beginning of the evening and said to make sure I kept her water glass full, and as far as I know, she let me pour one glass of wine but never sipped it. I threw away the whole glass at the end of the evening. It seemed a shame, too. It was a lovely wine."

I glanced over at her, thinking of what I'd said to Rafe. "If the host was a financial advisor and the dinner was that exclusive, were there interesting men at the table?"

She looked annoyed. "Obviously. I'm sure at least one or two of them were single. But there was this one very annoying woman who insisted on coming back to the kitchen to extend her compliments to the chef."

Her face was so sour, I suspected she hadn't much liked this woman.

"I didn't think anyone ever actually did that in real life," I said. "I've seen it in corny movies. Even so, they send their compliments to the chef and then the chef comes out."

"I think that's what she intended to happen, but William is so bashful, he told me to tell her how gratified he was, which I did, and next thing Miss Flirtypants was back in the kitchen bothering us."

I stifled my smile. "Flirtypants?"

"Honestly, Lucy," she said, leaning so close I could smell her toothpaste. "I might as well have not been in the room. She stood right in William's personal space, and if you ask me, all her raving about his delicious cooking was nothing but a ruse. She barely ate anything on her plate. I swear she counted every calorie before she put a thing in her mouth."

I made a face. I already had a mental picture of this woman.

"And then, of course, that wasn't enough for her. She made a date with William for coffee so they could talk about some bogus event she's pretending that she's planning."

I didn't want to laugh at my cousin, but she was being a bit overdramatic. "She probably does have an event."

"Well, if she does, I can tell you one person who won't be waitressing."

"Good. Because you have a perfectly good job right here. And speaking of that, look at the new shipment of wools that arrived. You could help me unload them."

She let out a long-suffering sigh. "Really, Lucy, you can be so unsympathetic at times."

"I know. You should report me to the Bureau of Labor."

"No doubt you think you're very funny."

But she did stalk over towards the boxes and begin opening them. One thing about Violet, she not only knew the shop better than I did myself, but she was a much better knitter. Okay, she was lazy, but we managed.

While she unpacked the latest shipment, I got some of my mail orders ready. So many people had taken knitting up as a way to pass the time at home that I was inundated with orders. In fact, that part of my business was growing fast.

One of our regular customers came in and, as I had, fell in love with that herringbone carpet on the front cover of the latest Teddy Lamont magazine, and I happily pulled together all the wools and supplies for her.

"Make sure you bring it in when it's finished. I'd love to take a picture of it and put it on my brag wall."

She was delighted and left with a huge smile on her face, especially when I confided that I was making that same rug myself. Violet might laugh at me, but how was I ever going to get better if I didn't keep practicing? Besides, I was friendly with some extremely good knitters who were only too happy to help me when I got confused. And, as I liked to tell anyone who would listen, mistakes were what made a project unique. And my knitting was extremely unique.

While we were working away, Nyx was happily snoozing in her basket in the front window, and I had a feeling of genuine contentment. It had been creeping up on me slowly, but I suddenly felt like I was where I was meant to be in the world. For someone who'd spent so much of her life being carted around from archaeological dig to archaeological dig and always feeling out of step with the rest of the world because I was different, I felt like I'd found my place.

The door opened, and I glanced up to see the witch Forest Sprite, aka Leo, walking in the door. *Well, take that, Violet.* Not only did he want to see her again, but he was so keen, he'd come into the shop to find her.

I said, "Violet, you have a visitor."

Then I could have bitten my tongue. I sounded like somebody's coy great-auntie when a boy showed up at the door with a box of chocolates in the 1950s. Violet obviously thought the same thing when she glared at me. Then she tossed her hair back and looked bored. "Oh, hello."

"Hi. I was in the neighborhood. Have you got time for lunch?"

I could see the war going on in her face. Yes, she wanted to go for lunch, because who wouldn't rather sit around eating food they didn't have to cook than unpack wool, but she also didn't want to look too eager. Finally, vanity won out. She said, "I'm sorry. I can't at the moment."

"Right. Sure. You're working. No worries. As I said, I was in the neighborhood." He headed to the door and then turned around. "What time do you get off? Do you fancy a drink at the pub?"

Oh, this was much better. A few hours of advance notice was definitely better than an impromptu invitation.

She squeezed the skein of wool in her hands a few times like it was a stress ball and then nodded. "All right. I get off at five."

"Great. I'll see you then." Then he raised a hand and said, "Catch you later," and he was gone.

"Well, that was good," I said. "He's totally smitten."

She sighed. "I suppose. It's all about being a witch, though, for him. I mean, yes, it makes us unique and interesting, but I have other things I'd like to talk about. All he wanted to talk about was spells and my powers and whether I thought this book was better than another one. As though I get my magic from books."

"Then I suggest you lead the conversation in the pub this evening. Let him see you have other interests, and maybe you can find out what his are. That's what dating is, you know, finding common ground with the other person."

Like I had so much experience.

"I suppose you're right. I'll give him a proper chance."

"That's the spirit. Or should I say *sprite?*"

She glared at my terrible pun. Who could blame her?

We went back to what we'd been doing. A couple of customers came in, including Clara and Mabel, two of my favorite vampires. We were having a vampire knitting club meeting tonight and, knowing them, they'd have finished all their projects by ten o'clock.

Clara's eyes lit on the newest Teddy Lamont magazine, and

she said, "Oh, what a lovely rug. Wouldn't that be nice beside my bed?"

Mabel agreed that it would. I said, not without pride, "I'm knitting one of those myself."

There was a strained pause and then they both burst out laughing.

"No. Really, I am."

"Dear, that's quite a complicated pattern. Are you sure you're ready?" Clara asked gently.

"No." I wanted to pout. Maybe I'd never be ready. Maybe I was destined to live my life as the knitting shop owner who couldn't knit. The butt of jokes from my staff to my vampire knitters.

Mabel came over and patted my hand. "Never mind. We can help you if you get stuck."

Actually, that's what I'd been planning all along.

"Don't get too far ahead of me before tonight," I begged them.

Mabel bought the lime green wool I'd accidently ordered, misreading the code and thinking it was forest green. I'd been contemplating dropping the price in half just to get rid of it, but she was delighted.

"You so rarely have lovely, bright colors, Lucy. This is exactly what I was looking for. Won't it make a lovely jumper."

I couldn't look at anyone else in the shop, alive or undead, as I pictured her in an entire sweater in that hideous color. "You won't get lost," I said with as much diplomacy as I could manage.

She scooped up balls and balls and then said, "And enough for a skirt, too, I think."

Oh, dear.

She looked at Clara, sounding very excited. "And don't you think if I knitted a pretty knit snood, I could put some nice pink flowers on it?"

"I think that would look lovely, dear."

They went off perfectly happy, and I wondered if we'd soon be reading about this strange creature appearing in the wee hours around Oxford, looking like Thoroughly Modern Milly had gone radioactive.

When the door opened again, to my surprise it was William, and with him was a woman about his own age who looked very pleased to be standing by his side.

William had the look of somebody who's been staring at the sun too long. He came over to me. "Lucy, I want you to meet Felicity Stevens. Felicity was at the dinner on Saturday night. We've been having coffee together, and she told me how much she's always wanted to learn how to knit. What a coincidence, as we were only next door. I was delighted to tell her we were beside the best knitting shop in Oxford and had to bring her right here."

As happy as I always was to welcome a new customer into my shop, I could feel waves of jangled energy coming from Violet. It was like live wires zapping at my skin. She came forward. "Felicity, what a surprise." She didn't sound thrilled.

Felicity was blond, nicely dressed and had one of those posh accents that made her sound as though she had a head cold. "Oh, hello. Why, you're the waitress from the other night. Sorry, I can't remember your name." There was an unspoken end to that sentence which went something like, "I can never remember the names of the hired help."

William, who didn't seem to be picking up the complicated undertones, looked absolutely delighted to see Violet. "What a good job you're here, Vi. Between the two of you, I know you and Lucy can help Felicity get started." He looked so pleased to have three women he liked all launched on a common project. So sweet. So misguided.

I didn't know what to do, so I decided to treat Felicity Stevens like I would any new customer. "Do you have much knitting experience?"

She looked startled by the question. "I've never knit a stitch in my life. My nanny used to knit when we were children. But when William was telling me about you and your darling little shop, I knew it was exactly what I needed to fill my lonely evenings." She glanced longingly at William as she said it as though she were hoping he'd offer to fill them for her.

I knew plenty of single women who enjoyed evenings alone with their knitting and their cats. Felicity Stevens did not look like one of them. I don't know what made me think she'd be found out on the party circuit rather than quietly knitting at home in front of a fire. I just knew.

But the tiger can change his stripes, I reminded myself. No, actually, I think that was the whole point of that fable. The tiger can't change his stripes. However, if Felicity Stevens wanted to spend money in my knitting shop, I wasn't going to stop her. If she never knit more than a row, that was nothing to do with me.

I began my usual session that I had with brand-new knitters, and within a couple of minutes, William said, "Right, then, I'll leave you ladies to it. Lovely seeing you again, Felicity. I've got your number. I'll be in touch."

"I can't wait," she said, beaming at him. With a wave to all of us, William left.

I'd have gone back to a discussion of the best needles for the beginner, the best wools, and naturally, I'd have sold her on our beginner knitting class, but the door was barely shut behind him when she said, "Isn't he absolutely wonderful?"

I blinked at her. "Who? William? He's very nice."

"He cooks like a dream."

"He does," I agreed. "Now, if you're interested in starting with a garment–"

She put a hand on my wrist. "How well do you know him, Lucy?"

I really didn't want to be interrogated about William by a stranger. Especially now that Rafe had confirmed he was a wealthy man. "Hardly at all."

She turned to Violet. "And you? You must know more about him, seeing as you work for him. I mean, what's he really like?"

"What's he like?" I could see Violet getting ready to say something most likely rude, so I hastily answered the question myself.

"William's an excellent chef, as you've noticed. Otherwise, he's more an acquaintance than a friend. Now, did you decide on the wool?"

Obviously seeing her chance to escape, Violet beelined for the back room, where she noisily began opening more of the boxes that had arrived that morning.

Twenty minutes later, Felicity Stevens left my shop with a large bag of purchases and hopefully not too many answers to her extremely nosy questions about William. Violet had stayed in the back room. However, as soon as the bells rang announcing that our only customer had left, my assistant came stomping out of the back room.

"You didn't have to be so nice to her. You practically put on the kettle for tea and asked her to be godmother to your children."

I was taken aback by the aggression. "Violet, this is a knitting shop. She came in to buy knitting supplies. What was I supposed to do? Throw her out?"

"You didn't have to encourage her to linger. She's insufferable." She struck a pose with her nose in the air. "Of course, our nanny used to knit, when she wasn't out grooming my pony and polishing my solid gold doll's house." She'd said it in a pretty good imitation of Felicity's voice, so I struggled not to laugh.

"Anyone's allowed to knit. What's really going on here? Is it because William seems to like her?"

She got all huffy at that. "I don't like her. Call it my witch's intuition. Or my woman's intuition. Some kind of intuition is telling me that woman is not someone we need in our space."

CHAPTER 6

*T*he next morning, Violet arrived late for work. This was nothing new; she considered anything within ten to fifteen minutes of her start time to be punctual. I greeted Violet cheerfully, and she glared at me. She was dressed all in black, a long black cardigan over a black shirt, a long black skirt and black boots. Both in attitude and garb, she reminded me of Hester on one of her bad days.

"How did it go with your date? The one from Witch Date?" I guessed that might be the source of the mood.

She blew out a breath and slumped back against a wall of wools. "Dismal. I'm afraid I behaved rather badly. He's just so annoying, and he's not a proper witch at all. Not like you and me. I don't think he has any powers. He likes the idea of being a witch. He was acting like a fanboy, wanting to know all my secrets."

Witchery, like every other pastime, drew its wannabes. Usually, Violet was more generous.

"I put up with it for as long as I could stand, and then I asked him some pretty searching questions that he couldn't answer. Naturally, I told him I had no time for fakes. That he was a complete poser and he could go on Plenty of Fish like all the other mortals or I'd report him to my coven to be dealt with."

Ouch.

She shrugged. "As I said, I behaved rather badly. I was going to send him an apology, but he's taken his profile down from Witch Date."

"I guess he took you seriously."

She got a bit huffy. "Well, I did the world of witches a favor then."

I knew she felt guilty, but it was a trying day, with her in a bad mood and me trying so hard to be extra nice to the customers that I ended the day with a headache.

That night, I gave myself a good talking to. I couldn't let my assistant ruin the atmosphere in the shop like that. I decided if she was bad-tempered the following day, I'd have to say something. Nyx patiently stared at me while we role-played. I played me. She played Violet. I only hoped Vi would be as placid if I did have to reprimand her. Though I doubted it.

I was ready to nip any bad attitude in the bud the next morning when she arrived.

But when she came into the shop, she stood inside the door unmoving. She held something in her hands and was staring at it. From the other end of the room, it looked white and ceramic. I wondered if it was a knitting bowl. From her usual spot in the window, Nyx let out a very strange howl and jumped out of the window embrasure and onto the floor. She stared at Violet with her back arched, her mouth open in a silent hiss.

What on earth? Then I turned to look at Violet properly. She was standing stock still with a shocked expression on her face. That wasn't a knitting bowl. It was a pale object with decorations of some sort.

"What is that?"

"You tell me? And what was it doing right in front of your door?"

I walked closer and then finally made out that the pale-looking thing she was holding out was a skull. Not human, as I quickly ascertained, but some kind of animal skull. There were markings on it, something that looked like scrawled writing in a language I didn't recognize, and some feathers and smaller bones dangling from it.

I understood why Nyx had freaked out. The thing was giving off a nasty vibe.

"I have no idea."

She shook her head at me. "Why didn't you move this? You'll put off all your customers if they see a bleached skull in the front of the shop."

"I never come in the front way. You know that. I live upstairs. My commute is the run down the stairs into the shop. Then I open the blinds, turn on the lights, open the cash register, unlock the door, and I'm done."

"Well, you'd better start looking outside from now on. That front entrance is the customer's first impression, and this isn't giving a very good one."

Nyx had finished having a fit. Now she stood by the door up to the flat and meowed. *Thanks for the support, Nyx*, I thought as I opened the door and she scampered once more upstairs to our flat.

I came closer and looked at the skull. Violet put it on top of the desk as though she couldn't stand to touch it anymore. Not that I blamed her.

"Could someone have dropped it?" I asked. It was a pretty stupid question, but how else did a skull find its way to a storefront on Harrington Street? "Maybe it's part of a class at Cardinal College and a student lost it somehow." Cardinal

College was up the street from us, and we often had students walking past.

She shook her head, looking worried. "I don't think that this ended up in the doorway by accident."

"You mean someone put a dead animal head outside my door deliberately?"

I admit, immediately my thoughts went to the vampires. Was this some sort of weird vampire joke? Their sense of humor could be very peculiar.

She shook her head. "Look at the markings. It's witchcraft. A curse of some sort."

I looked more closely and saw what she meant. Pentagrams had been drawn crudely in black and some letters that made no sense.

"But why? Who?"

We both stared at the skull. "Two excellent questions."

"What did they use to draw this stuff? Crayon?" I tried to sound sarcastic to hide my growing unease.

She was a lot more experienced a witch than I was, and I wasn't surprised when she said, "That's not crayon. I suspect it's drawn with ashes and a burned wand."

"That sounds creepy. What kind of ashes?"

"Depends what was burned."

I turned to her. "What should we do with it?"

"I don't know."

"Can't we throw it away?" I wanted this thing far away from me. Its energy was nasty.

She put a hand to her heart. "Don't even say such a thing. I feel the negative energy coming from it. I'm just not sure what kind or how deadly."

Now it was my turn to put my hand to my heart. "Deadly?"

"Haven't you been studying your grimoire at all? All those lessons Margaret Twigg's been teaching you? Do you think witchcraft is nothing but snapping your fingers and having the wools magically tidy themselves up?"

Okay, that was my favorite spell and probably the one I was most proficient at because I practiced it the most often, but I knew perfectly well there was dark magic as well as light. I just preferred to concentrate on the light.

"Well, I'm not having it sitting in the middle of my cash desk. If it scares the customers away, that's a curse right there."

"No. We can't leave it here. We'll have to take it upstairs to your flat."

"What? No."

"What about taking it downstairs to the vampires?"

"But what if it's from them? What if it's a practical joke and all we do is encourage them to play more by reacting?"

She tapped her fingers on the desktop and regarded the skull more closely. "I don't think this was made by vampires. Look at those marks."

We were still staring at the thing when the door opened. Without even thinking, I took the skull and shoved it in the cupboard underneath my cash desk and slammed the door on it before anyone else could see it.

"Good morning," I said a shade too brightly as two older ladies came into the store. They explained that they lived in a small Cotswold village and a friend had sent them my newsletter, so they'd decided to come and see for themselves. I was super excited whenever this happened. I might not be the greatest living witch or the greatest living knitter, but I was turning out to be a pretty handy internet marketer. Those couple of years of business college back in the States hadn't gone to waste after all. I welcomed them, and soon they were browsing happily. Then another customer came in.

As soon as her back was turned, Violet leaned across the table and whispered, "You're going to have to move the skull."

I nearly gagged. Her breath was foul. I tried to step back out of the way, wondering how to tactfully suggest a breath mint. I needed to move a dead animal skull from under my cash register and keep Violet out of speaking distance of my customers.

Before she could offer to help anyone, the two ladies headed for the door. "It's a lovely shop," one said to her friend in a low voice, "but there's a smell."

"I noticed it too," her friend whispered back. "Pity."

Oh, this was not good. I had to get that dead thing out of here. I knew my shop didn't smell, but non-magical people would often explain a bad atmosphere as a smell. It was a way of interpreting things that were outside their realm.

While we continued with our day, I didn't have any better idea than Violet did what to do with an animal skeleton's head that had been left on my doorstep. I felt it there, though, a low-level annoyance. Like a hornet's nest that you knew was nearby because you could hear the low buzzing of the insects and you were wary any minute that you'd accidently bump into it and find yourself in a world of hurt. So I was careful around the cash desk. I didn't have to spend too much time at the cash register, as no one was buying. Even people who weren't witches were probably being put off by the force field of negativity that thing was putting out. I really needed to get rid of it.

When the third person in a row had walked out without buying anything, Violet looked to me. "Do you think someone's put a curse on your business?"

I hadn't thought about that. "But who would do that?"

"I don't know. Maybe a rival knitting shop. You said yourself that all your internet marketing is paying off. People are driving a long way to come to your shop. Maybe some other knitting shop owner's watched too many of their customers drive past their shop on the way to yours."

"You think there are that many witches that own knitting shops?"

"Maybe. You don't need to be a witch, though. You could always buy a curse."

I knew that was true, but I hated to think about it.

One thing I knew for sure, I was getting rid of that skeleton head before I opened the shop again tomorrow. I didn't want to lose any more business.

I needed that thing out of my space, and the sooner it was gone, the better.

CHAPTER 7

I tried to get Violet to take the skull home with her, but she refused. She also refused to destroy it or let me throw it away. I didn't want to take it upstairs to my flat or downstairs to the vampires. Who else might store it for me?

I went through the witches I knew. Margaret Twigg? No. I didn't trust her. For all I knew, she was the one who'd sold it to a knitting shop rival. My great-aunt Lavinia and Violet's grandmother? No. She was getting on in years, and I didn't want to upset her.

While I didn't want to put it in the subterranean nest where some of our local vampires lived, I thought maybe Rafe would take charge of the skull for me. That put the cursed thing far away from me and in safe hands. I phoned Rafe and asked him to come to the vampire knitting club meeting a few minutes early because I had something to discuss with him. I didn't want to talk about curses and skeleton heads on the phone. It sounded creepy and weird. No doubt he was accustomed to creepy and weird, but I tried not to be.

So about quarter to ten that night, Rafe strolled into my shop where I was waiting for him. He came right up and searched my face with his sharpened gaze. "Lucy, are you well? You sounded a little perturbed."

I made a noise too much like a snort to be considered lady-like. "Perturbed barely covers it. Look what Violet found outside the shop this morning," I said, opening the cupboard beneath my cash register so he could look. I didn't want to touch the thing; it gave me such an unpleasant feeling.

He bent down and peered into the dark cupboard. The white of the bone picked up what little light there was and seemed to glow with it. Unlike me, Rafe had no compunction in touching the skull. In fact, he reached in and picked the whole thing up. He tilted it this way and that, studying the symbols and words.

"Curious."

Talk about master of understatement. "Curious? That's what you have to say?"

"I haven't seen one exactly like this in some years. They were quite popular a hundred to two hundred years ago."

"What? Putting dead animal heads in front of people's shops?"

He turned to me and shook his head. "No. Hexes done this way." He looked again. "There might be something like it in the Pitt Rivers Museum. You'll find a lot of old curiosities there."

"Hexes? You think this is a hex?"

"Undoubtedly. Don't you?"

Here he had me. I was the witch. Shouldn't I know if something was a hex or not?

He said, still studying the object, "*Hexe*. It's German for witch, you know." Just one of the many things I didn't know.

"You think a German did this?"

He smiled slightly. "I don't. Merely that an object like this signifies a witch is probably involved."

"Well, I didn't think some animal died out on the sidewalk and decomposed before morning."

"A goat, I think."

It was bad enough knowing it was an animal carcass. Now I actually knew it was a goat. "Poor Billy."

"The goat as a symbol is associated with evil. I don't like this, Lucy. What have you done to annoy people?"

Why did everyone immediately think it was my fault?

"I don't think I've done anything. Violet thought maybe it was my newsletter. I've developed more business from small towns in the area and all over the world. She wonders if maybe it's a rival knitting shop owner who wants me to suffer for stealing their business."

He looked skeptical. "Is business that good?"

I immediately ruffled. "It's not bad." But I knew what he meant. Cardinal Woolsey's Knitting Shop was never going to hit the Fortune 500. It wouldn't even hit the Oxford 500. But it was a tidy little business, and I was quite proud of how well I was doing.

He looked more closely. "I don't think this is about business. It's personal. Have you upset someone personally?"

"Not deliberately." In fact, the only person I could think of who had a beef against me was him. He'd asked me to marry him, and all I'd done was think about it obsessively without coming to a decision. Though Rafe wouldn't put a hex on me. And if he did, at least it would make my decision for me. I was never going to marry a man who would hex me.

He picked it up and carried it over to where I kept a rack of ready-to-buy knitted garments, which the vampires kept stocked. "Are you planning to buy it a sweater? Maybe a hat?"

"Come and look in the mirror." I kept it so people could see themselves in the knitted garments they'd tried on. I never liked being around mirrors and Rafe. As I looked at the skull, which appeared to be floating, I was once more reminded of the vast differences between my undead beau and me.

"Come closer. Look at the words."

I did, and then what I'd thought was random scribble turned out to be a phrase written in English. I'd had trouble deciphering the words because they were written backward.

Grow ugly, wither and die.

I shivered. No wonder he believed it was personal. I tried to think of who might want to hurt me. "Sylvia's not exactly my best friend since she almost got me killed."

He shook his head firmly. "Sylvia's trying to make amends, in her unfortunate manner. Anyway, she's not this subtle. No, I don't think a vampire's behind this."

"You think it's a witch."

"It certainly took a witch to make this and imbue it with the magic."

At the same time we both said, "Margaret Twigg."

He looked at me. "Have you been doing something to annoy the head of your coven?"

The truth was I was always doing something to annoy the head of my coven. I either didn't study hard enough or didn't take my magic seriously enough or didn't spend enough time with my grimoire. I said, "Just standing near her and breathing seems to annoy Margaret Twigg."

He put the head down on the table where I keep magazines and books, and it made a clicking noise. "You know perfectly well that Margaret Twigg is annoyed with you because she senses your power. Hers is waning, and yours is growing every day."

This wasn't a compliment. Or at least, not one I wanted to hear. I was a witch, and it was not a path I had chosen, but I was trying to learn. However, I wasn't an ambitious witch. I had no desire to replace Margaret Twigg as the head of our coven or anything else. I much preferred to keep a low profile, and okay, I definitely used the tidying-up spell, and perhaps I'd been known to mutter a few words into my mirror when an unfortunate pimple showed up. Other than that? I was doing the best I could to learn my craft while still running a business.

"Will you take it away for me?" I asked him. "Just having it here stopped people from buying anything in the store today. My sales were abysmal."

With *Grow ugly, wither and die* floating in the atmosphere, no wonder they were fleeing.

He looked quite surprised. "You kept the skull in the store all day?"

"What would you have had me do with it?"

"Put it somewhere safe until you can remove the curse."

"I can't keep it here; it's driving the customers away. I can't throw it away. I need a safe place to hide it until I figure out how to disarm it."

"Fair point. Yes. I'll keep it for you." He gave it a long look. "Though, if you've no objection, I think I'll find a sturdy shed on the grounds. I don't particularly fancy it in the house."

"Oh, yes, so long as it's safe and secure, keep it as far away from you and anyone you like as you can."

He nodded. "Though, as I'm sure you know, hexes are directed at a certain person usually."

"Right," I said as though I knew much about it at all. Clearly, I was going to have to put my athame studies aside and start working on hexes. It was never-ending. I no sooner felt like I was gaining mastery of one subject when another one thrust itself under my nose that I had to study. It was exhausting work being a witch.

"Right, I'll just take this and pop it in my car. And then I'll come back for the knitting club meeting. What are you working on tonight?"

I showed him the magazine cover. Rafe wasn't one to show

shock easily, but his eyes did widen slightly. "You're knitting that?"

"Is there any reason why I shouldn't?" I asked, full of cool dignity.

I could see him fighting his smile. "No. Not at all."

I grabbed my supplies and headed into the back room. I'd make sure I sat beside my grandmother, who could be counted on to quietly guide my knitting when I got into trouble.

I had a horrible moment when I wondered if that animal skeleton hex might throw me off my knitting game.

And fast on the heels of that thought was another. How would I be able to tell?

CHAPTER 8

While Rafe took the goat's skull out to his car, I gathered up my herringbone carpet. I had hoped to have a better start on it before being thrown into a knitting circle where the collective experience of the other knitters was in the thousands of years. But between hexes, a temperamental cat, and a sulky employee, I hadn't exactly had a lot of extra time.

I didn't like the idea that someone had put a hex on me. I was nice. And knitting wasn't exactly the kind of profession that created enemies. It had to be a mistake. I couldn't help but think that someone had dropped that skull outside my door by accident. No doubt there was someone out in Oxford wishing evil on someone else and it was bouncing back to me by virtue of proximity.

I liked that theory a lot better. No doubt it was some love-struck student who wished evil on a rival. Or a kid who'd gotten a bad grade trying to curse one of the dons. Throw a bunch of super-smart, highly stressed twentysomethings into a town like Oxford that was steeped in history and drama and magic, no wonder they got a little carried away. Trust an Oxford student to take revenge the extra mile.

I'd talked myself into a much better frame of mind when Rafe returned, and after making sure the blinds were closed and the door properly locked, we headed to the back room. Most of the knitters had already gathered and were sitting either gossiping or starting to work on their projects.

Mabel had made a start on her green sweater, unfortunately.

I wished I'd thrown that wool away the minute I saw it rather than leave it around to tempt her. Poor thing. I'd never seen anyone who combined such excellent skill with such terrible taste. Still, she was cheerful, and while the rest of the vampires kept looking away as though the sight of that bright green wool hurt their eyeballs, she chattered along looking delighted with herself and the growing expanse of something that looked more like green ooze from a science-fiction film than a color anyone would want to wear.

Beside her, Clara had already knit several inches of the herringbone rug. I was excited to see it in progress and immediately went up and inspected her work. She patted the empty seat beside her.

"You sit here, Lucy. I've done this for you. I've just given it a little bit of a start. All you have to do is continue along, following the pattern." She gave me her open magazine and pointed to where she'd got to. Then quietly, so no one who wasn't staring at us would notice, she took my bag and drew out the tangle of wool, the creased magazine and went quietly to work. I was so grateful, I leaned over until our shoulders were touching and whispered, "Thank you."

She twinkled at me. "Our little secret."

Of course, it wasn't like I could suddenly, magically pick up where she'd left off. I studied the pattern until I was nearly cross-eyed. And then I decided I'd just take it on faith. I'd do the best I could, and if I had to unpick a few rows, it wouldn't be the first time. And it certainly wouldn't be the last.

Sylvia and my grandmother came in together. Gran came over and gave me a hug, as she always did when she saw me. Her eyes widened as she saw the project I was working on. If she could tell that there was six inches or so of perfect knitting followed by a lumpy, uneven row that was already messing up the pattern, she didn't say anything. Only commented on how pretty the pattern was and how nice the rug would look when it was finished.

Sylvia glanced at me and then away again. Then she came deliberately towards me.

"Lucy," she said. "That's a lovely rug you're working on."

"Thank you," I said coldly.

Maybe I was being rude and childish to carry my grudge on this long, but she had nearly gotten me killed. I'd get over my mad one day but not today.

She was always so imperious and acted very much like the celebrated movie star she'd been in the 1920s that it was strange to see her humbled and actually sucking up to me. Okay, I was really enjoying it.

Before we started our usual show and tell, Mabel said in a voice she didn't bother to lower, so everybody could hear it, "Lucy, Clara and I were wondering if perhaps you've got a vermin problem upstairs."

I was so shocked, I dropped my knitting in my lap.

"What? I couldn't have. Nyx is very particular about that sort of thing. The first thing she does every morning is go sniffing around the edges of the shop and make sure no mice have dared come into her space."

"I think perhaps she's killed something and it's hidden some-where. We could smell death."

Oh my gosh. Trust those vampires and their super-sensitive

noses. I glanced at Rafe. He said, "I smelled it too when I went into Lucy's shop. It wasn't a dead mouse. It was the skull of a goat."

Unlike me, with less than thirty years on the earth, vampires were rarely shocked.

"Really? What sort of a goat?"

This was Alfred. It seemed a very odd question to me, but Rafe said, "I should think it was just an ordinary farm goat. Something local to the area."

"Odd place to keep a goat's skull, Lucy."

"I didn't put it there," I hastened to assure them. "Somebody dropped it outside of my shop."

Rafe said, "Placed it there, I should think." Everyone was looking at him now, so he continued, "It had magic symbols and a curse drawn on it."

"A hex?" Alfred asked.

"I believe so."

Now they all looked at me as one. "Who have you upset, Lucy?" Silence Buggins wanted to know. "You have to be so very careful, a young person alone as you are. And a shop-keeper too. In my day, a young lady was never left alone where a gentleman might come upon her and cause her to have a spasm."

You wouldn't think a woman who insisted on dressing in Victorian garb, including a very restrictive corset, had enough breath to talk as much as Silence Buggins did. You'd be wrong.

I could barely open my mouth to tell her and the rest of them that I hadn't done anything when she launched into an extremely boring story about when she herself had worked in a button shop.

"I was hexed once," Sylvia interrupted in her theatrical way, tilting her chin up in a pugnacious manner.

"No," Gran said looking shocked. "Who would hex you?"

Sylvia's lips went rigid before she relaxed them enough to speak. "I rarely mention her name. She's dead to me."

"We wouldn't know her anyway," I said. "She's probably dead to all of us."

Her eyes flashed, and then she remembered that she was still groveling, so she merely said, "Nevertheless, I was hexed by a jealous rival. She harmed my career and stole roles that should have been mine."

She looked around the room. "Swedes. I never trust them."

A Swedish actress had hexed her? Maybe I was no expert on the silent film era, but I'd known Sylvia long enough to hazard a guess.

"Are you saying Greta Garbo hexed you?"

Her eyes flashed once more. "I never mention that name."

I'd heard of professional egos, but this was ridiculous. "Greta Garbo was the most famous silent screen actress in the world."

She looked coldly furious. "Exactly. And how do you think she got those roles that made her famous? It should have been me. It would have been me, if she hadn't hexed me."

I suspected that the so-called hex was nothing more than greater talent, maybe some luck, but I didn't want to push my luck with Sylvia. Not when we weren't exactly getting along.

There was silence, and then Gran, who was trying to heal the breach, said, "Do you know how Lucy might be able to break the hex?"

"If I knew how to break a hex, my dear, it would be my face you'd see when you watched *Grand Hotel*." And with that, she sat down and picked up her knitting.

There was a pause. "Perhaps I could investigate," Theodore said. He'd been listening intently. "If Lucy doesn't know who's angry with her, how will she know who's cursed her?"

This was true. "It's very nice of you, Theodore, but I really don't think the hex is directed at me. I don't have any enemies."

They all turned instinctively to look at Sylvia. In spite of what I'd said, I glanced her way, too. As though aware of the attention, she looked up, and her eyes flashed with fury.

"I would never stoop so low. How dare you."

"No, no. No one thinks it's you," Theodore said, not helping at all.

Rafe spoke into the strained atmosphere. "Lucy wondered if it might be a rival knitting shop owner. Her newsletter and digital marketing seem to be having some effect in bringing knitters in from other areas."

"It's possible, I suppose," Gran said. "I'm very proud of you, my love. You've really taken our little knitting shop into the modern age."

Her flattery warmed me. I wanted my grandmother to be proud of me. And I wanted Cardinal Woolsey's to do well, for her sake as well as mine. But not if it meant getting cursed.

"I don't know."

Gran said, "You must ask Margaret Twigg."

"I don't want to. Anyway, how do we know it wasn't she who made it?"

"She may well have made it. It's who I'd go to if I wanted to put a hex on someone. Maybe she'll tell you who bought it."

"I don't know."

"Well, it's not like she can do anything worse to you. You've already been cursed." Then she thought for a second and said, "But just in case, take Violet with you."

CHAPTER 9

The next morning, Violet arrived with a Band-Aid across her chin.

"Cut yourself shaving?" I asked.

"Oh, very funny. No. I've got the most horrid pimple."

"That sucks. Don't you have a potion for breakouts?"

"I've tried everything. Nothing works. I think my grandmother's got something. I thought I'd go around tonight and get her to take care of it for me."

"That's a good idea." I really hoped Great Aunt Lavinia had a cure. That spot was getting larger, and redder, by the minute.

She came towards me, but the sewer smell of her breath preceded her. I blinked. What had she been eating?

I set her to work in the back room again packing up orders. I couldn't tell her that her breath was eye-wateringly foul. But I couldn't keep her busy in the back room all day either. Then I had a brainwave. I'd buy a couple of muffins from the Miss Watts' tea shop next door. I'd put a little spell on one of them to sweeten her breath.

So I ran next door and picked out two bran muffins and brought them back with two cups of coffee. We did treat ourselves sometimes to food and drinks from next door, so it wasn't out of character.

I took her coffee and muffin into the back room, having imbued it with the best I could do for a breath-cleansing spell. She might smell a bit powerfully of mint for a day or two, but surely that was better than smelling like an outhouse that's been in the sun for too long.

"Lovely. I didn't have time for breakfast this morning. How clever of you to know." Even those few words had me stepping back and trying to hold my breath until I was out of range.

"I'll have mine at the cash desk. Just in case someone comes in."

And please let that spell work quickly.

I'd barely taken my first sip of coffee when I heard a scream from the back room. And then a muffled curse.

"What is it?"

"What was in that muffin? I've broken a tooth."

"What?"

The Miss Watts were in their eighties, but they were excellent cooks. Had they accidently dropped something in the batter?

I went to the back, and sure enough, there was a muffin with a bite through it and a shocked-looking Violet holding her front tooth in her hand.

"Oh my gosh. This is terrible."

"It's my front tooth!" she said, sounding kind of muffled because of the missing front tooth. "See if you can put it back for me."

I didn't think she was suggesting glue. She wanted a spell. The breath-cleansing one hadn't worked, or perhaps she hadn't eaten enough of the muffin. I nodded, centered myself, which wasn't easy, as I was nervous and also had half an ear out for the front door.

"Quickly," my cousin said, making me instantly more nervous.

I had talents and some skill. It was a matter of focus and intention, I reminded myself. Focus and intention. No time for candles and a magic circle that always brought calm and focus. Nyx had refused to come downstairs this morning, even though the skull was gone, so I wouldn't have my familiar's help. On the plus side, Violet could blend her power with mine so we'd be like a super witch. And hopefully magic superglue.

"Hold the tooth where it belongs," I instructed her. She did and then I breathed in and out slowly, picturing her smiling a perfect, fully toothed smile.

I felt my body growing warmer and my fingers began to tingle. In my limited experiences, spells mainly helped a witch to focus. I managed an impromptu rhyme:

Spirits of the east, west, north and south,
Repair this broken tooth within Violet's mouth.
Knit the pieces tight, her perfect smile to see.
So I will, so mote it be.

When I opened my eyes, Vi gingerly took her hand away from her mouth, then carefully smiled. The tooth looked as good as new. Just as I was feeling pretty good about myself, however, it fell off again, bouncing off her lower lip. She only just caught the tooth before it fell to the floor.

She let out a sigh. "You really must work on your magic."

I didn't want to argue with someone who couldn't properly argue back, but I'd felt the magic working.

Why had her tooth fallen off again?

"Now what do you suggest?" she asked, staring at the tooth in her hand.

"Have you got a dentist? I'm sure they'll let you have an emergency appointment."

"Let's hope they can do a proper job." She sighed, a great

gust of breath that made my eyes water. It was so bad, I actually stumbled back a step. She didn't seem to notice.

"I'll drive there right away. They'll have to get me in." And she handed me the tooth. "Here. Put this in a damp towel or something."

I went into the back and used some of the water from the kettle to dampen a paper towel and wrapped up her poor tooth. Then I took it back out to her. "Do you want me to drive you?"

She shook her head. "No. You stay here. It doesn't hurt. It's just horrifying." I felt she was blaming me for her misfortune, but I hadn't baked her muffin, just bought it.

Weirdly, I did feel guilty. And worried that maybe Florence and Mary Watt weren't coping as well as I always thought. "Call me and let me know how you get on."

She nodded and dashed out. I spared a moment of pity for the poor dentist who'd be working near the halitosis capital of Oxfordshire.

I wasn't busy enough that I really missed Violet for the rest of the day. I even had time to do a bit of cleaning. It must have been a while since I'd swept the floor from the amount of Nyx's black hair that was all over the place. I got the broom and began to sweep up and then I noticed there were streaks of pink and purple. This wasn't Nyx's fur I was sweeping up. It was Violet's hair.

What on earth?

I was looking at the mass of hair I'd collected in the dustpan, wondering, when Theodore arrived, coming through from my back room so quietly I didn't hear him. He'd come up from the trapdoor in the back room that led down into the subterranean tunnels that in turn led to the underground complex where a number of the vampire knitting club lived.

He was beside me before I even noticed he was there.

"You look lost in thought, Lucy."

"I'm not sure that hex was meant for me."

I shared with him my theory that Violet was the one who was suffering a string of misfortunes. "Her breath is absolutely foul. She came into work this morning with a massive pimple on her chin, and she broke her tooth on a muffin."

"That could have been a string of unfortunate occurrences," Theodore said. It was one of the reasons he made such a good detective. He didn't ever jump to conclusions.

I held out the dustpan for him to see. "And she's losing her hair."

"I can certainly see why you have discerned a pattern. And there could well be one. But this is your shop and residence. I think it would be prudent for us to look at who might want to put a hex on you."

I nodded. "That's true. But she was the one who picked it up and brought it in. I live upstairs. I would never have seen that skull until I left the shop, which might not have been until lunchtime or even later."

He gave my statement his full attention. "So you're suggesting that whoever put the hex on Violet knew that she worked here and would be the one most likely to stumble across it?"

When he put it like that, it didn't sound like a compelling theory, but I was perfectly fine and Violet was falling apart in front of my eyes.

He looked around. "Where is Violet now?"

"She went to the dentist to get her tooth stuck back on."

Since there were no customers at the time, he took advantage of our chance to talk frankly and brought out his notebook. "Think very carefully. Has anything happened lately to upset you? Do you have any enemies? Could you have inadvertently made someone angry with you?"

I shook my head. "We all know that Sylvia's angry with me. Well, she was angry with me. Now I'm angry with her."

"It's not Sylvia."

"That's so unfair. How can you immediately discount her when you won't entertain the thought that Violet could be the victim? Who's jumping to conclusions now?"

Theodore had a face like a baby that never thinned down as it grew into manhood. He looked chubby and sweet and cherubic, which was probably another reason why he was such a good detective. People tended to discount him. But behind that sweet expression was a steel-trap mind. He turned his mild, blue gaze on me.

"I'm not supposing anything. I interrogated Sylvia quite thoroughly. I am satisfied she had nothing to do with this."

"Okay then. So long as you're not jumping to any conclusions."

"I try very hard not to do that. Now, can you think of anyone who's angry with you?"

I wrinkled my face. Not just my nose, my whole face. "Margaret Twigg. I had an email from her this morning telling me off for falling behind on my witch lessons. It would be just like her to put a curse on me to see if I could break it."

"Good." He wrote Margaret Twigg's name in his notebook. "Can you? Break the curse?"

"I tried to fix Violet's tooth, and it fell off again. And the skull isn't even on the premises. That is some powerful magic. I don't think I can break it without knowing more about the hex. Especially who put it on me. And I might need some extra help."

"Who else could want to harm you?"

I had been thinking about it, but I really didn't have any enemies that I knew of. Not living here in Oxford anyway. "Maybe a customer who wasn't happy with their merchandise?

But I've got a perfectly good return policy. I can't think of anyone who's not been a satisfied customer."

"What about neighbors?"

I shook my head again. "Charlie and Alice in Frogg's Books wouldn't be married now if it wasn't for me. The Watt sisters are like honorary grandmothers. I get my groceries at the grocery store at the top of the street. I can't think of anyone who would be angry with me."

"And Violet?"

Aha, he did think it could be Violet.

"She met this guy on Witch Date. He called himself Forest Sprite, but when he came here, he said his first name was Leo."

"Forest Sprite, aka Leo," he mumbled aloud as he scribbled notes.

"Yes. They went on a date, and then they went on a second date and she was pretty mean to him. She basically accused him of not being a real witch. Said she'd report him to the coven. She was in a bad mood about something else. Then she said when she went to write to him to apologize, he'd taken his profile down."

Theodore raised his head from his notebook. "Taken his profile down? This was an online dating site?"

"Oh, sorry. That's a really important part of the story. It's a dating site specifically for witches on the dark net. It's called Witch Date."

He glanced up at me. "W-I-T-C-H?"

I nodded. "That one."

"That does sound promising. I don't suppose she knows his surname?"

"I don't think so. I could give you a description."

He shook his head. "Hester's very good with computers. I'll see what she can find out." He tapped his pencil on his page and said, "I think I'll get Hester started on that right away. You should go and see Margaret Twigg."

"And ask her if she's put a hex on me?"

His full, baby lips curved in a smile. "If she wants you to pay more attention to your magic, she'll probably be pleased that you even noticed the hex."

"She'd have to think I was a really useless witch if I didn't even know when a hex had been put on me."

I didn't want to see Margaret Twigg. I never wanted to see Margaret Twigg. But he was right. I'd better find out what she knew.

"I'll see if Violet can come with me."

"Excellent idea. I'll be in touch."

He turned to head back and stopped. "Oh, this is nice."

He'd come across the new batch of a wool/silk blend from the Shetland Islands. The colors were named after wine regions and had a richness and softness that I loved. It was the batch that Violet had been unpacking when she had the unfortunate incident with her tooth.

"It is nice, isn't it? That Chianti you're holding would make a lovely cardigan. And I've got these really nice leather buttons that would go well with it."

The pair of us spent a happy ten minutes pulling together enough wool for one of the Teddy Lamont cardigan patterns he chose. And he agreed with me that the buttons were perfect. I might not be a great knitter, but I had an eye for style. I sent him away, not only with clues in a case of hexing but a knitting project as well. Two birds, one stone.

CHAPTER 10

I got busy then, and for a full hour, I actually wished my assistant was here. But she wasn't, and so a couple of my customers had to wait a few minutes to be served. Nobody seemed to mind. In fact, two of them got chatting over the baby wool, and it turned out they were both expectant grandmothers. Not only did they happily pass the time waiting for my attention; when I was ready for them, I had a hard time getting theirs.

At last I had the shop to myself again. I immediately texted Violet to see how her tooth was.

"Got emergency appointment. Fixed now," she texted back.

She didn't say anything about returning to the shop, and frankly, with that bad breath, I didn't want her to. I texted back and asked if she'd go with me to Margaret Twigg's after work.

She agreed that she would, and so I said I'd pick her up at her house.

When five o'clock came, I shut the shop as usual and went upstairs, where I found Nyx sleeping on the couch. The second I appeared, she leapt off the couch and stood by her food dish, meowing. "That's boredom eating, babe," I informed her. "You should come downstairs to the shop. You like it there."

Not while the place is cursed. The words appeared in my head, but I didn't think those were my words. They were Nyx's.

"I'm getting rid of the hex. Promise," I replied. And the sooner, the better.

I fed her and freshened her water and then headed out to pick up Violet. Normally, I would have taken Nyx along with me to alleviate her boredom. She was my familiar, after all. But after a rather unfortunate incident when Margaret Twigg had catnapped Nyx, I never took her near the place.

So I grabbed a large roll of breath mints and headed out.

When I got to Violet's cottage, I suffered a shock. Two more Band-Aids decorated her face, but the one on her cheek wasn't big enough to cover up the profusion of bright red pimples that stood out on her skin. And her left eyelid was swollen and half-shut and seemed to droop down towards her mouth. Her mouth itself was swollen, but I suspected that was something to do with the broken tooth and whatever the dentist had done to fix it.

I didn't say a word. She must know she wasn't looking her best. She glared at me as if daring me to comment on her appearance, so naturally, I didn't.

"Ready to go?" she snapped at me.

I nodded and got back into the car. Brightly I offered her a mint, and she glared at me. "I've just had dental work," she snapped at me again.

Being in this close proximity in the car, the burst of halitosis made my eyes water. I didn't care that the January evening was freezing. I unrolled my window and determined to drive as fast as I possibly could. Fortunately, Violet's cottage wasn't very far from Margaret Twigg's.

Margaret Twigg's cottage was exactly what a witch's cottage should be. Made of stone, set back from the road, sitting on its own. It had once been in the middle of the great Wychwood Forest, but now there wasn't very much forest left. Still, it was isolated, and even though it was a charming cottage, it had an atmosphere. Even if you didn't know Margaret Twigg was a witch, you'd probably suspect she was.

I had called ahead to tell her we were coming, and she flung the front door open before we even got to it.

"What a welcome surprise," she said, ladling sarcasm over the words. "I'd begun to think you'd forgotten all about me, Lucy." No doubt she'd have continued for some time in that vein, except she caught a glimpse of Violet and recoiled. "Violet. Whatever have you done?"

"I haven't done anything." It didn't come out quite that clear because of the tooth and swollen mouth problem.

"You've been cursed, my girl."

Aha. I had been right.

Violet acted like that possibility hadn't occurred to her. "Not me. Lucy. Someone put a hex on Lucy, but I was the one who picked up the skull they left outside the front door of her shop."

Margaret Twigg's piercing, blue eyes moved rapidly from her face to mine. "Have you got it with you?"

I shook my head. "It's at Rafe's. Locked away in a shed. It was only in my shop for a few hours, and it scared away all the customers."

"Naturally. Look what it's done to Violet. I suppose that's why you're here? To get me to do your work for you."

She wasn't the most gracious of witches. "Could we come in?" I didn't really feel like standing out in her garden talking about the curse.

She didn't seem best pleased to let us inside. She looked at Violet as though my cousin might be contagious with a deadly disease. "Don't touch anything."

"What have I done?" she said again.

"It's not what you've done, my dear, it's what's been done to you. And why. You've made an enemy."

Violet mumbled an answer, and Margaret Twigg stared. "No one's offering you an enema, you odd girl. Have you been drinking?"

"She said she doesn't have any enemies," I said, feeling like an interpreter at the UN.

"Her face tells a different story."

"We're trying to figure out who it was." I told Margaret Twigg about the Witch Date. "He calls himself Forest Sprite. But his first name might be Leo."

Margaret Twigg looked like she might spit cockroaches out of her mouth, she was so mad. "You went on Witch Date?" She glared at Violet, who in turn glared at me.

"Hanks nor rabbing." Which I interpreted as "Thanks for blabbing." Oops.

Before Margaret could berate Violet any more, I said, "We have to get rid of this hex. And the dark witch from the dark net sounds like the most likely culprit."

Margaret Twigg looked both annoyed and slightly amused. "I have never known anyone who has worse luck with dating than you, little sister."

Violet hung her head, and two more strands of long, black hair floated down onto the flagstone floor of Margaret Twigg's kitchen. The fire was burning away in the enormous fieldstone fireplace, and a mid-size cauldron was steaming with some mixture that was bubbling away. I could smell mint and licorice, and I was fairly certain I smelled cannabis.

"Tell me about this skull then," Margaret Twigg said to me.

I glanced at Violet, but I wasn't having a lot of trouble recalling the object. It was imprinted on my memory. "It was the bleached skull of some kind of goat, we think, with magic symbols drawn on it and some feathers hanging down from it."

"What symbols?" Margaret Twigg snapped at me. It reminded me of the way a fourth grade teacher had snapped multiplication table questions at us. I still got startled if anyone asked me what five times four was.

"One was a pentagram. One was something that looked like a thumb; a crow, I think; and a message written backward."

"Interesting." She walked over to stir her cauldron and then took a glass jar of white powder from a shelf and sprinkled some into the bubbling liquid, whereupon it boiled furiously before she murmured a few words and it quieted again.

"Did you make it, Margaret?" I asked it in a casual way. It was a technique I'd seen Theodore use. Throw in the pointed question as though it was perfectly benign.

It didn't work on Margaret, of course. "I sell any number of hexes, Lucy. I couldn't possibly say."

Oh, and that told me.

"Have you sold any recently? To a guy with bleached hair who calls himself Forest Sprite?"

She shuddered visibly. "I can't imagine I'd sell anything to anyone calling themselves Forest Sprite."

She hadn't answered the question though, had she? More significant, she hadn't asked what the message on the skull said.

Violet made a furious sound, and we both turned in time to see her spit her broken tooth into her hand.

"Can you fix it?" Violet asked, holding out the once more broken tooth. She sounded desperate.

Margaret shook her head. "It's the curse. The easiest solution is for the person who hexed you to remove it."

"But we don't even know where Leo is. He took his profile down."

"Then you must reverse the hex yourselves."

"You're a powerful witch. Can you reverse it?"

She crossed her arms under her meager chest. Her gray, corkscrew curls seemed to dance in front of my eyes as though she'd stuck a finger in an electric socket. Her eyes grew sharper and bluer.

"Lucy. You don't take your training seriously. You don't respect your own power or the coven or the fact that I keep warning you dark forces are on their way. And now you expect me to reverse a hex? This is an excellent test for you. Do it yourself."

I felt my jaw drop as my mouth opened.

Violet would have done the same if she could have. "But what about me?" The bad eye was closed all the way now and drooping even more. And the way her hair was drifting off her head, she was going to be bald soon.

Grow ugly, wither and die. I hadn't told Violet about that nasty little backwards-printed phrase, but she was definitely growing ugly. How long until she began to wither?

"Yes. You can certainly work on it. And preferably while Violet's still got one good eye and a bit of hair left."

"What do we do?" I asked, feeling desperate.

Margaret Twigg rolled her eyes. "You'd know how to reverse a hex by now if you'd been keeping up with your lessons. That's why they're so dangerous. A powerful witch can turn the hex back on the person who sent it. If you're really annoyed, you can double its power."

"Cool." Not that I wanted to cause anyone misery, but someone had definitely tried to cause Violet misery, and she might be a bit annoying, very competitive and a lackadaisical employee, but she was my cousin. I was definitely fond of her.

"I suppose you're not going to tell us how we reverse a hex?"

She gave me that thin, superior smile that always made my teeth grind together. "No. I'm not. Go home like a good witch and read your grimoire. And you can read some of those books I've been recommending for your library. And you can set yourself a magic circle and meditate within it and see what comes to you."

"Fine." Then I looked around her well-stocked pantry. If you ever needed eye of newt or bat wing or milk of a slug collected under a full moon, this was the place to come. "Is there anything I'll be needing that you have here?"

She glanced at Vi, looking worse by the minute and with her hand clasping her tooth, then went into the back room and returned with a small bottle of black powder. "That's soil from the grave of a hanged witch. You'll need it. Have you black candles?"

I nodded.

"Then you'd best get started." Naturally, nothing was ever free when Margaret Twigg was involved. She wanted twenty-five pounds for this tiny vial of what was probably dirt from her back garden, but Violet was in a bad way, and I was willing to try anything to help her.

Margaret Twigg hesitated and then crossed to where she had a planter of herbs growing in the windowsill. She picked several and handed them to Violet.

"Chew them well. Swallow the juice but not the leaves."

Violet took them, looking rather surprised. "Will that help my tooth heal faster?"

She shook her head. "No, dear. But hopefully it will help that dreadful halitosis."

She put a hand in front of her mouth. "I've got bad breath?"

"It's not your fault. It's the hex. But unless you want Lucy passing out while she's driving you, I suggest you chew those. And perhaps breathe out the window."

Before we left, I had one more question. "Can't we just remove the hex?"

Margaret Twigg gave me that sarcastic, superior look she so often cast my way. "Not unless it was you who cursed your cousin. Besides, reversing a hex is so much more satisfying, don't you think?"

"What about our oath to first do no harm?"

She gave me her thin smile. "I like to finish that with an unspoken codicil. Do no harm unless provoked first."

I was pretty sure that wasn't in any witch's manual I'd ever seen. However, since Margaret Twigg was so easily provoked, I didn't inquire deeper. Instead, we thanked the older witch and left.

"I can't believe I've been hexed," Violet said. I didn't like to tell her, but another horrific-looking pimple had sprung out on the end of her nose.

"I know. What an awful thing to happen."

"I am never dating again. That's it."

I felt so bad for her. "You don't know it was Leo. Not for sure."

"Who else is mad at me?" She shook her head, which she probably shouldn't have done because a cloud of hairs drifted away from her scalp. "I shouldn't have been so mean to Leo. That's what comes of angering another witch."

While I thought she could have handled Forest Sprite a little more diplomatically, I also thought he was a real jerk to make her suffer like this, and I told her so.

"I'm going to go home and study the family grimoire. Hopefully there's something in there about reversing a hex. In the meantime, talk to your grandmother. Lavinia's been a witch a lot longer than we have. Maybe she's got some ideas."

"I don't want to tell her. She'll be so upset."

I didn't say it, but unless she wanted to be bald and toothless and covered in pimples, with only one eye to be able to survey the damage in the mirror, we really needed to pull in every helper we had. And that was before she got to the wither stage of the hex.

Ultimately, I was even willing to go back to Margaret Twigg and beg for help. But not until I'd given hex reversal a good try myself. Much as Margaret annoyed me, she had a point. If I was going to accept my powers and be a part of this local witch community, I was going to have to try a little harder.

Before Violet got to the final stage of the hex.

The bit that said *Die*.

CHAPTER 11

J dropped Violet off at her cottage and then returned home in a pensive mood.

I drove my little car around the back of the building, so I entered my home through the back entrance in the stairway that led up to my flat, thus avoiding the shop. However, I'd barely climbed two steps before I knew I was not alone. This wasn't as unusual as it should have been, considering I was an independent adult and this house belonged to me. Gran or Sylvia or really any vampire who felt like a visit seemed to think it was perfectly okay to waltz in and out of my home.

They usually at least rang the bell first or knocked if coming by way of the shop. However, if I wasn't home, they'd come on in and settle down to wait.

I hoped it was Gran waiting for me, as she'd been a witch in life. Though, now that she was a vampire, her magic had faded, and I sensed she was increasingly vague about the spells she had once known so well.

But it wasn't Gran waiting for me. It was Theodore, and with him was Hester. Sitting together on my couch, they made the oddest couple. Theodore was serene and chubby and always had a cherubic look on his face. Hester was a perennial angry teenager with long, black hair who usually dressed all in black, and her most normal expression was a scowl. Her mood had improved lately though, now that we had a young vampire who she seemed to enjoy spending time with. But Carlos was a university student busy with his studies. He hadn't embraced knitting the way the rest of them had.

He was a beginner like me, which made me really warm to him, and Hester got quite patronizing when she showed him where he'd gone wrong and corrected his stitches. Still, if it wasn't the grand romance Hester was hoping for, at least she had a friend closer to her own age.

Even more surprisingly, she'd recently started to team up with Theodore in his private investigation practice. She was a whiz on computers, and she had absolutely no compunction about breaching people's privacy. She hacked into systems for fun when she was bored. I supposed it was better than a steady diet of soap operas in the afternoon.

She no sooner saw me than her scowl deepened. "There you are. We've been waiting ages."

As though we'd had an appointment and I'd stood them up. Theodore hastened to say, "I hope you don't mind us dropping by, Lucy, but Hester's found your mystery man."

I'd been about to snap at Hester. Now I quelled the impulse, irritation turning to surprise. "You did? Already?"

My astonishment made her preen. "It wasn't very hard. Silly fool's using the same IP address. So I had no trouble at all linking Forest Sprite's closed account on Witch Date with Robin Goodfellow's brand-new one."

I rolled my gaze. "This guy's not big in imagination, is he?"

"Just as well for us, I believe," Theodore said. "It made Hester's job tracking him down much easier."

She glared at him as though he'd dealt her the most

appalling insult. "It wasn't easy. You try it, you old git. You couldn't even find your arse in the dark, never mind the dark web. Then try tracking someone down who's doing business there."

He immediately set about trying to make her feel better. "My apologies, Hester. You're remarkable. I couldn't possibly manage without you. I wasn't criticizing your skills as a computer expert so much as Robin Goodfellow's lack of them."

She settled her back once more against the cushion of the chintz sofa in the living room. "He could have given me a bit more challenge," she conceded.

I added my mite of praise. "That's great, Hester. We think he's the guy who put the hex on Violet."

"What are you going to do? Now we've found him."

Hester had me there. I hadn't imagined they'd find him so quickly. And now that they had, I didn't have a step two of the plan. I needed a crash course in how to break a hex. I toyed with the idea of asking Hester to search on the dark web but stopped myself. The thought of Hester mixing it up with witchcraft sent chills down my spine.

I'd been standing all this time, so I put my car keys in the little bowl where I kept them and placed my bag on the floor. Nyx must have heard me come in, as she made her stately way down the stairs from where she'd no doubt been sleeping on my bed. After rubbing herself against my legs, she graciously allowed me to pick her up, and I settled, with Nyx on my lap, opposite the other two.

Nyx didn't say a lot, but somehow just being with her seemed to sharpen my wits. I was pretty certain some of my thoughts were actually planted by my familiar. Either that or I was a lot smarter than I'd ever believed myself to be.

So even as I sat there, the solution popped into my head. Margaret Twigg had said I could reverse the hex, or the person who put it on Violet could remove it. Seemed like door number two was going to be both quicker and easier. "The site's called Witch Date. I'm a witch. I'll send Forest Sprite, now Robin Goodfellow, a message and see if he'd like to go out with me. Then I'll convince him to remove the hex."

Even Hester looked impressed. "Not bad, Lucy. You'll never be as good as me and Theodore, but you're not a completely hopeless amateur."

"Thank you," I said, hoping I sounded truly grateful for the compliment and not sarcastic.

Nyx purred loudly as I stroked her from the top of her head to the end of her back in long, smooth motions.

Anyway, I couldn't afford to annoy Hester. I needed her cooperation. The way Violet's condition was deteriorating, we probably didn't have a lot of time. "Can you help me set up a profile?"

She blew out her breath through closed lips so she sounded like a motorcycle backfiring. "Easy as."

I wasn't one to put off until tomorrow what would get me out of researching hexes in my grimoire tonight, so I said, "Could we do it now?"

"Don't see why not."

I fetched my laptop and handed it to Hester. She got busy while Theodore and I discussed how we might trap Robin Goodfellow and then convince him to lift the curse.

At one point, Hester glanced over and said, "I could do it. Give me five minutes with him." Her white teeth gleamed when she smiled.

"Hester, you know we've moved on from the old ways," Theodore reminded her gently.

"Yeah, but Robin Goodfellow doesn't know it."

I felt vaguely alarmed, but Theodore shook his head and gave her an indulgent look. He did seem like he managed her well. And if she grew too annoying, Rafe could always get her to behave.

"Do you need any details?" I asked Hester to bring her attention back to my dark web dating profile. She shook her head. "I took a look at some of the other profiles on the site. It shouldn't be difficult to fake something passable. I won't put anything that identifies you."

"But remember, I only want a date with one witch. We need to target the profile exactly to whatever he says he's looking for."

She pushed a couple of buttons and showed me his page. I recognized him from his picture. The same bleach-blond hair, that same thin face, but he was wearing some kind of black robe and had displayed his pentagram necklace on the outside of it.

"Yep, that's him."

She turned the screen back to herself and read aloud. "Robin Goodfellow. I'm from a long line of Gloucestershire witches, with a branch of the family in Cornwall. One of my ancestors was a healer at Tintagel Castle. Women without magic bore me. I'm looking for my kindred sprite, a woman who wants to stand barefoot under a full moon with me. To blend our two gifts into the purest magic.

"I also enjoy a good game of darts, cozy evenings around the fire, and a good footy match. If you think we might be fated, wave your magic wand in my direction."

I nearly choked. "He's got to be joking."

She glanced up, and I could see she was in complete sympathy with me. "You should read some of the other ones. They're even worse."

"And I'm supposed to write a profile as lame as that?"

"Yes."

"What about a picture? I can't put a picture on there. He'll recognize me. He came and picked up Violet from Cardinal Woolsey's." I turned to Hester. She looked a lot more like a witch than I did, with that long, black hair and the black clothes. "Can't we use your picture?" They both stared at me balefully, and I mumbled, "Sorry."

"Don't worry about the photo," Hester said. "I'll amalgamate several photographs. He'll never know it's not a real person."

She was so impressive, it was scaring me.

"Good," Theodore said. He wasn't particularly excitable, but he did enjoy the thrill of the chase. "Now we must write Lucy's profile."

"I could pull up the old one I used in Boston. On eHarmony."

They both stared at me.

"What? It got me a few dates."

I was beginning to feel like Violet. My luck in the romance department hadn't been all that exciting until I'd arrived in Oxford.

"First, we must come up with a name for Lucy."

This could be fun. My very own witch name. I said, "Well, he keeps on about the moon. Though, now that I think about it, Violet was Mistress Moon. We'll have to have something else."

"Goddess of the Moon?"

Hester made that motorcycle backfiring noise again. "There must be a hundred of those on this site. Don't witches have any imagination?"

"Spellbinder." Even as I said it, I was worried Robin Good-fellow might think I had something kinky in mind.

"Luna?" Theodore suggested.

"From which derives the word lunatic," Hester said with relish.

Who knows how long we'd have continued trying to come up with the right name if someone hadn't rung the bell? I answered the intercom, and Rafe's deep voice answered me.

"I'm glad you're home. Can I come up?"

"The more the merrier." Before he could ask what I meant by that, I pressed the button that would open the downstairs door. He arrived upstairs and blinked when he saw my companions.

"We're writing a dating profile for Lucy on Witch Date," Hester informed him. She might have been around for hundreds of years, but sometimes she sure acted like a teenager. How had her common sense not evolved in the time she'd spent on earth?

I quickly glanced at Rafe and was in time to see a look of tragedy instantly stifled. I'd never seen someone go from hopeful to hopeless so quickly before. And it pulled at something deep inside me.

"It's not for real," I said quickly. "We're trying to catch whoever put that hex on Violet."

He'd regained control of his features by now anyway. And as smooth and urbane as always, he stepped forward. Nyx immediately abandoned me and flirted with him outrageously until he picked her up. Then he sat down beside me on the couch.

"I think you need to fill me in. Why is Lucy going on a witches' dating site?"

I left Theodore to explain all the details to him. He listened in silence and then said, "Empress of the night."

A shiver of recognition went down my spine. Hester nodded. "Not bad."

Theodore nodded. "It's not got the word moonlight in it but something so much more."

"It's from a poem," I said. I felt rather smug. I might not be as well-read as the man who dealt in antiquarian books and had been reading and studying them since Shakespeare's time, but I'd taken introduction to poetry in college.

He nodded. "Longfellow. One of your poets, Lucy." And then he quoted, in his rich, deep voice, "She walks the terraces of cloud, Supreme as Empress of the Night."

I looked at him. "I thought you'd argue that it was a terrible idea for me to do this."

"Do I believe it's a poorly conceived plan for you to confront someone who is capable of putting a powerful hex on you? Why would I think that?"

Oh man, I hated it when he did that cold, superior sarcasm thing.

"I have to do something to help Violet. Anyway, she says he's not a real witch at all."

"He sounds like a right twit," Hester said.

"How will you get him to remove the hex? Assuming he chooses you out of all the witches on the dark net to date. And that he's the one responsible for the hex."

And thank you for that. I hadn't really thought it through, but rapidly I did. "Maybe I could slip a truth potion into his drink and then challenge him."

"And if he admits to being spiteful and revengeful, wanting to hurt Violet, then what will you do?"

"I'll get him to take the hex off. Or at least tell me where he bought it. Because I really don't think he has the power to do it himself. I'll make him remove the curse."

I pictured the scene. There could be some uncomfortable moments. But I wasn't without power. "And then I'll do my forgetting spell on him. I've had plenty of practice, especially at the beginning when I first came here and Gran kept forgetting that she was dead and appearing in the middle of my shop. Can you imagine how many nervous breakdowns there would have been among the knitters of Oxford if I hadn't learned how to do that spell that made them completely forget the last few minutes?"

Nyx was purring so loudly that she was embarrassing herself.

"I have a couple of conditions before I'll agree to being part of this."

Since nobody had asked him to be a part of it, it was a bit presumptuous, and maybe I would have acted huffy if I hadn't seen that moment when he'd thought I was off on a dating site without even giving him an answer to his marriage proposal. What kind of witch would do that?

Theodore asked what his conditions were, and Rafe said, "This date will happen in a public place, and Lucy will not go alone."

"Naturally, she won't go alone. I fully intend to be in the vicinity in case she needs help."

Theodore was becoming as bad as Rafe, always thinking he had to protect me. "The worst the guy could do is attempt to put a hex on me. And he won't be able to. So I don't really know how you could stop him. You're vampires, not witches."

"Lucy," Rafe said in a long-suffering manner. "Somehow, wherever you go, you wind up in trouble."

Hester snickered, but I flared up. "That is so unfair. I don't ask to get in these horrible situations."

"Nevertheless, you do."

It was hard to argue against reality. I could blame Sylvia for sending me into harm's way, or bad luck, or a hundred other excuses, but the truth was I did seem to draw danger the way Rafe's black trousers were currently attracting Nyx's fur. It wasn't a bad idea to have backup in case Robin Goodfellow had more power than I was giving him credit for.

"Fine," I said, sounding uncomfortably like Hester. "Agreed."

"Now we have to build me a profile that's going to appeal to somebody who calls himself Robin Goodfellow and thinks the height of excitement is to stand under a full moon with his beloved witch."

"What an amateur," Rafe said.

My thoughts exactly. "I'll put everything cheesy that people think is true of witches."

"Read me the profile," Rafe said.

Hester obligingly read it again. Rafe said, "He craves acceptance. He's looking for someone magical who will make him feel magical as well. I suspect you're right, Lucy. He doesn't have any powers of his own. He wants to be powerful by association. It's the only chance he has. We must feed into that. Tintagel, of course, is associated with King Arthur."

Now that he was with the program, Rafe was an excellent ally. He was brilliant and had a vast knowledge of human behavior, having been around so long.

He said, "Start with your lineage, the way he has. Pedigree seems to be important to him."

"I can't tell him about my family. He's the kind of fool that might try to show up to coven meetings."

Hester sneered. "Not your real lineage, stupid. Make it up."

The ghost of a smile flickered across Rafe's lips. "That was what I had in mind, yes."

"What about saying she's descended from Morgan le Fay, the enchantress in the King Arthur legend?" Theodore suggested.

"That's good. Yes," Rafe agreed. "But is it too obvious?"

"You could tell him that your people come from Glastonbury," Hester offered.

I shook my head. "That's too close to the truth." Oh, but Glastonbury gave me an idea. "Glastonbury is where King Arthur is supposedly buried. What if we let him think I know secrets no one else does?"

There was general enthusiasm for this idea, so I dictated and Hester typed. "I can trace my magic line back to Merlin. They say King Arthur is buried at Glastonbury. But I know that isn't true. I know where he is. On our second date, I'll take you to King Arthur's final resting place. But first I need to know I can trust you. Our first date should be in a coffee shop."

"No," Theodore said. "A pub. He mentioned liking pubs and darts."

"Right. That's better." I glanced at Hester. "In fact, maybe you should mention darts. Or football."

Rafe shook his head. "It's too obvious. I think what Lucy has there is perfect."

Hester had typed what we'd suggested, and then she turned the computer so I could see it. The photo she claimed to have created definitely looked like a real person.

"Are you sure that isn't a stock image from some photography site?" I asked.

"No, it is not. I took Violet's face, since we know he liked her enough to go out with her, and I crossed it with... Well, I'm not telling you all my secrets. Trust me. He'll go for it."

The woman had long black hair, eyes that slanted slightly upwards in the corners, a full, sensual mouth, and somewhat of a challenging gaze. As Robin Goodfellow had been, so was she wearing all black. She didn't have anything as obvious as a pentagram around her neck but what looked to me like an ammonite fossil. Nice touch.

We all agreed that my listing was perfect, and then she uploaded it to the site.

"We'll give it till tomorrow night, and then you can ping him, Lucy," Hester said. "If you send him a message now, even he might smell a trap."

I agreed to be guided by her, and then obviously realizing that Rafe had come to see me, not them, Theodore very tactfully got up and said that they should be going. Before they'd got two steps, there was a ping on my computer. Hester's eyes lit up, and she ran back to the laptop.

"Ha. You've got your first one."

"My first what?"

"Your first interested witch. He sent you a black rose."

"How flattering."

"It's like sending a wink on this nutty site."

"Is it Robin Goodfellow?"

"No. It's Master of the Wands."

Oh man. It was going to be a long evening, I could tell. Five minutes later, there was another ping. "Midnight Jester."

"Are these guys for real?"

"Lucy, they're on a dark net site called Witch Date, and you have to ask that question?" Hester looked at me like I was a few petals short of a black rose.

Good point.

"I don't know about this," Rafe said. "They sound like escapees from a lunatic asylum."

There was another ping. "No, really, I can't take any more of this," I said. "I am shutting that thing off."

But Hester looked as delighted as I'd ever seen her when Carlos wasn't around. She turned the computer my way and said, "Robin Goodfellow just sent you a black rose."

CHAPTER 12

"*I* got a black rose," I said, tickled.

"If only I'd known you were partial to them," Rafe said in a dry tone.

"Ooh, he sent you a message, too." Hester was extremely proud of herself. As she should be.

"Read it aloud," Theodore said. He was leaning forward, trying to see the screen, and then he gave up and sat back down beside her.

"Greetings, Empress. Your profile called to me, like a beautiful owl sitting high in a yew tree."

Rafe made a sound of disgust. "Foolish puppy. Doesn't he know that the lonely hoot of an owl is the harbinger of death?"

And I thought if this was an earlier age and these vampires weren't well-fed, foolish Robin Goodfellow could be announcing his own imminent death. At least these days, all they punished foolish humans with was scorn.

"Read on," I said.

"I always knew King Arthur wasn't in that grave. I've stood there in that very spot and felt the emptiness underneath my feet. I hope I can intrigue you enough to get to a second date.

Shall we meet for a first one tomorrow night at The Flag and Bear in Oxford? It's probably the most central place for us to meet."

I felt slightly alarmed. "How does he know I live in Oxford?" I glared at Hester. I should have paid more attention to what she was doing.

"Relax. I said you live ten miles outside of Oxford, but I didn't name a town."

Okay. In England, ten miles was like three states' worth of distance in the US.

Hester said, "Should you play coy? And wait until tomorrow to reply?"

The other three of us all shook our heads in unison. "He's hooked now," Theodore said. "Saying you know where the real King Arthur is buried was brilliant. He's so excited at the thought of gaining some inside knowledge, it hasn't even occurred to him you could be stringing him along."

"I agree," I said. "Also, I don't know how long Violet's got. That hex is nasty. The quicker we remove it, the quicker she'll get her looks back. Tell him I'll meet him tomorrow night. And he should bring a black rose."

Hester snickered at that, then quickly typed up my reply and sent it before I could change my mind.

It wasn't five minutes later that he responded he'd be delighted. How was 7 p.m.?

"Perfect," I had Hester reply on my behalf. "Blessed be."

He echoed my reply, and then I said, "And shut that thing down before any more crazy witches get hold of me." I was worried that one of the men from our coven might write to me. How embarrassing would that be? At least I wasn't using my real picture, but if Hester could track down somebody from their IP address, who knew who else could do it?

I ARRIVED at The Flag and Bear half an hour early for my witch date. I'd done this deliberately, as I wanted to be in the position where I could control both where we sat and how the whole date went down. With three vampires hovering around, I wanted to make sure that I was the one with my back to the wall so that Forest Sprite, aka Robin Goodfellow, had to look at me and wouldn't notice he was under surveillance. Just on the off chance that he really did have magic powers, how would he not notice three vampires pretending not to stare at him? Even a non-magic person might figure that out. Theodore and Rafe, I was pretty sure could be cool, but Hester was hard to miss and not the most subtle of vampires.

I walked in alone at six-thirty feeling oddly jumpy. The thing was, the minute he saw me, he was going to know who I was and that I'd posted a fake profile. Well, obviously it was going to be very clear to him very quickly that this wasn't a real date and my whole purpose in meeting with him was to stop that hex.

I glanced around and, as expected at six-thirty on a Wednesday evening, The Flag and Bear was busy with students, tourists, and locals who'd come out for a pub dinner. If this were a normal date, it would be nice to stay for dinner, but I was pretty certain we wouldn't be extending this date for the rest of the evening. Not a chance.

I began walking around looking for the table that would give me all the advantages I wanted. Fortunately, the pub wasn't full. As I was scanning around looking for my perfect spot, my gaze fell upon a table where two women were chatting and giggling.

I might not have given them a second glance except that one of them was eating shepherd's pie, my absolute favorite meal. The other had fish and chips. My second favorite.

There was a bottle of wine on the table, and from the way

they were giggling and leaning into each other, I suspected there wasn't much of it left. It might not even be their first. As I glanced up, I realized I recognized the women. One was Felicity Stevens, the woman William had brought into Cardinal Woolsey's, as she wanted to learn to knit—the one who'd gone into the kitchen specially to congratulate him on his excellent meal.

The other was Jemima Taft, who looked similar, only a more polished version. They shared the blond, highlighted hair, and their dress style was similar, but while Sylvia would have been able to spot the designer right away, I could only guess that Jemima had spent about ten times as much money on her wardrobe as Felicity had.

I'd been in the wool trade long enough to recognize that the coat hanging over the back of the bench seat was cashmere, and I recognized the triangular logo on her handbag as Prada. I didn't think it was a knockoff.

Felicity's coat was a wool blend, and her handbag sported no designer calling card.

She must have felt me staring at her, for Felicity glanced up at me and blinked, as you do when you know someone but you can't remember for the moment where you know them from. I had the advantage on her. I smiled.

"Hi, Felicity. It's Lucy, from Cardinal Woolsey's. How are you getting on with your knitting?"

"Lucy," she said as though we were best friends. "Wonderful. Really, really wonderful. Well, I haven't actually started knitting yet, but the wools are so beautiful. I can't wait to begin."

Jemima Taft glanced up. "Knitting? You're taking up knitting?"

She shrugged expansively. "It seemed like the thing to do. You should try it. It's very relaxing."

"I could use some relaxation." She sipped her wine and then

said, "Oh, you're William's friend. You were quite right. He gave us a lovely meal. Didn't he, Felicity?"

"Lovely," her friend parroted, though I'd already heard her sing William's praises ad nauseam. Then she looked down at the table all prim and embarrassed.

Jemima laughed. "And William's been hot and heavy ever since."

"We've only had coffee. And one dinner." Since Saturday? That did sound hot and heavy. I'd have thought William would take things more slowly.

"What a good thing Gretchen canceled Saturday," Jemima said, "so I could invite you to the dinner."

"And I could do you a favor."

"Turned out well for both of us." Then Jemima seemed to notice me standing there as though she'd forgotten I was there. "Gretchen had a sick child. Or maybe it was her husband. No. She'd have come if it was only her husband. Must have been a child."

"You were furious," Felicity reminded her. "Absolutely foaming at the mouth."

"I had every detail planned to perfection. The right people with aligned interests and liquid assets. I couldn't have an empty seat at the table."

"So I stepped in to save the day," Felicity said grandly.

"After I informed you that two single and extremely rich men would be at dinner." She poured the last of the wine into Felicity's glass. "But you were more interested in the artist in the kitchen, you sly thing."

"It was William who introduced me to Lucy," Felicity said. "They're good friends."

"Lovely. And now you're knitting."

"I can't wait to get started," Felicity said, though I suspected it would be a long time before the wool came out of the bag. Not that I was one to judge.

"Do you get many young women knitting?" Jemima asked.

"You'd be surprised. I get all kinds. It's not just grandmothers, you know. Lots of the Oxford students knit. I'd say ten or fifteen percent of my clientele is men. Your friend's right. You should try it. It's a very relaxing hobby."

Honestly, how my tongue didn't turn black and fall out, I don't know, the way I trotted out sentences like that. But I knew lots of other people who did find it relaxing. I simply wasn't one of them. Maybe, if I ever actually gained some expertise in a craft I found utterly infuriating, I wouldn't have to spout other people's opinions as my own where knitting was concerned. If I told people what I really thought of knitting, I'd be bankrupt in a month.

Felicity leaned into her again. "I'll take you to Lucy's shop. You'll love it. It's so quaint."

I said, "We offer classes, too. That's a very good way to get started. You've got the camaraderie of other knitters who are also learning. Lots of people have become friends."

"I'll think about it." She smiled. "Will you join us for a drink? I must fetch another bottle." Honestly, she sounded like the queen at her garden party. Well, how I imagined the queen might sound at her garden party, since I had never been invited to one. And I bet this woman had.

Much as it would be fun to sit with a couple of women my age, I had to decline. "I'm meeting someone. But thank you."

"Another time," Jemima said, still sounding like a society hostess even as she slurred her words ever so slightly.

I headed into a different part of the pub and found exactly what I was looking for. A table for two tucked away slightly from any other diners but which gave me a good view of most of the rest of the pub. Once I had settled, Rafe quickly stationed himself where he could see me. Theodore was invisible—that's how good he was—and Hester was off scowling in another corner.

As I sat there at an empty table with nothing to do, I realized how stupid I'd been. I should have ordered myself a drink at the bar on the way. Now if I got up to get one, I'd risk losing this prime spot. The alternative was to sit here by myself at an empty table, which seemed lame.

Even as I was trying to decide what to do, Rafe walked over. In his hands was a long glass of some sparkling beverage with a lemon in it. It looked like a gin and tonic, though I suspected it wasn't. He didn't say a word, just slid the drink toward me and kept walking. Unless you'd been watching him the whole time, you wouldn't have seen him do it. I was grateful he'd so quickly remedied my predicament, and sipped my drink. As I'd suspected, it was sparkling water.

I heard laughter and thought it was Felicity and Jemima. On a different night, I'd have been happy to sit with them. I needed to make more friends with women my own age who weren't magic. I missed those girls' nights out. I was briefly homesick for the life I'd led in Boston. This didn't happen to me very often, but once in a while, I missed my girlfriends. I calculated the time difference. When I got home, maybe I could Skype or Zoom with a friend in the States.

It seemed a long time until my date got there. I pulled out my phone so I'd have something to do, but I didn't want to spend much time looking at it in case I missed him. He'd be looking for the woman Hester had invented, and I needed to catch his eye first.

He was on time, I'd give him that. Just about a minute before seven o'clock, I saw the man I had known as Forest Sprite, and then Leo, look around with a slightly eager, puppy-dog expression on his face. He was dressed in black jeans and a black pullover. The pentagram gleamed so brightly I suspected he'd polished it. He was carrying a black rose.

I almost felt bad for him that I was going to dash his hopes of meeting a hot witch and discovering the secret site of King Arthur's burial.

He glanced around, saw me sitting by myself and, as Felicity Stevens had done earlier, he got that slightly confused look of *Do I know this person?* And then I could see him trying to place me. I raised my hand and motioned him forward.

He looked around as though he might spot Empress of the Night and then, not immediately seeing her, came forward.

I said, "It's Lucy. From the wool shop? I think you know my cousin Violet."

He looked immediately wary and took a single step backward.

"You're here to meet me," I informed him.

He shook his head. "No, I—"

"Oh, you are. I'm Empress of the Night. And you're Robin Goodfellow."

He sat down then but still looked confused. "You don't look like your picture."

"Yeah. Sorry about that. I was worried if you recognized me, you wouldn't come."

"I probably wouldn't have. Your cousin's a bit mad." He had a frown between his eyes and perched on the edge of his chair, ready for flight.

"Not as mad as somebody who would put a hex on a woman just because a date didn't go very well."

He looked at me blankly at first, then annoyed. "Your cousin put a hex on me? That would explain my cycling accident." He lifted up his arm and pulled back the sleeve of his sweater so I could see a scrape that went all the way up his forearm. "Seriously, that woman is barking mad. I had to take my profile down." Then he looked sharply at me. "Yeah. I took my profile down. How did you find me?"

I gave him a pitying look. "We're witches, remember?"

That shut him up. If he was pretending to be a witch, he could easily suppose that we had those kinds of powers. And maybe there were witches who included computer hacking among their talents. I just didn't happen to be one of them.

"Nice try. It was you who put the hex on Violet. And I need you to take it off again. She's really suffering. I understand you being annoyed. She feels really bad about what she said. You taught her a lesson. Let it go now. Remove the hex."

He shook his head. "I don't know what you're talking about. You're as crazy as she is. I did not put a hex on that crazy witch." He stood up and went to leave but bumped into the broad chest of Rafe, who had completely broken with our script of staying in the background. Why was I not surprised?

Robin Goodfellow looked alarmed now. He tried to sidestep around Rafe, saying, "Excuse me," but Rafe merely moved so that once more he loomed over the poor man.

"I think you should sit down again," Rafe said.

Leo was looking quite panicked now. "What do you people want?"

Rafe answered, "My friend here wants your assurance that you will take the hex off her cousin."

"I told you. I didn't put a hex on anybody."

"Did you buy one?" I asked. Maybe I didn't love that Rafe had interfered, but he was definitely keeping Leo here so I could finish the conversation.

"No. I don't want anything to do with that crazy witch. I told you. I don't care what happens to her. She was horrible to me, but a hex costs money, and I've got better things to do with mine. She's not worth it." He gestured to the rose sitting forgotten on the table. "I'm moving on."

Rafe and I exchanged a glance. He sounded like he was telling the truth.

"How can I believe you?"

He held his hands up. "I'm not a real witch. Okay? I just think witches are really hot. I discovered this dating site, and I thought, why not?"

Rafe said, "We are witches. Very powerful ones. So unless you want to get on our wrong side, I would strongly suggest you tell us the truth."

Leo was sweating freely now. I could see Rafe's nostrils quivering slightly, whether in distaste at the rancid smell or some atavistic hunting urge, I wasn't sure.

I asked, "Then why is Violet suffering all the agonies of a hex? Do you know anything about a goat skull?"

He looked completely confused now. "Goat skull? No. I don't even eat meat."

Rafe and I exchanged another glance, and then Rafe said, "All right. You can go. But remember, we found you once. If we need to, we'll find you again."

And then, like a frightened hare, my date for the evening jumped up and ran, leaving his black rose behind.

Rafe picked it up and studied it. "I think he used spray paint."

"I think I believe him."

"I did, too. He's clearly not magic and I'd say not very bright either."

"Then who put a hex on Violet? Time is running out, Rafe. She's losing her hair. Her skin's a mess. One eye is swollen shut. She's lost a tooth. What if it's permanent?"

"Do you have to have the person who put the hex on her remove it again?"

I shook my head. "No. Margaret Twigg says we can reverse

the hex, send it back to the person who sent it, like unwanted mail."

"Well? Perhaps that's what you should do?"

I had a bad feeling about this. "I'm worried. It seems to me that when you reflect magic back, it can get even more powerful. And we're not even positive that the hex was meant for Violet. Maybe it was meant for me, but because she picked up the skull, she's the one who's ended up suffering."

"Do you believe that?"

"I don't know what I believe."

"You're worried about your cousin."

"I am. She drives me crazy, but she's family. I hate to see her suffering like this."

He said, "You look pale and worried. May I suggest, since I saw you looking with longing at other people's food, that we get you something to eat? You'll feel better after a good meal. Then we can work on reversing that hex."

"The thing is, if Leo did buy that hex and we reverse it, he could end up very ill."

"Then he really shouldn't have lied to you, now, should he?"

I couldn't argue with that. "If he did buy a hex, where would he have got it from? I don't think anyone advertises them. Margaret Twigg would sell him one in a minute, but she's not talking." And then I wondered who else sold hexes. "See if Hester can check the dark net. Maybe there is someone locally who's selling them."

"Good idea. I'll get her right on it. In the meantime, pick something from the menu."

I grinned at him. "I already did. I'll have a shepherd's pie, please."

"A woman of decision. I like that. Does William know about these plebeian tastes of yours?"

"You know he does. William makes excellent shepherd's pie."

"I'm glad to hear it."

Rafe sat with me while I ate my dinner. He told me that Theodore and Hester had already headed back to start searching out who might be selling hexes in our area. It struck me as a very dangerous side business for whoever was making and selling them.

CHAPTER 13

*R*afe offered to drive me home, but it wasn't a long walk from the pub to my place, and after I stuffed myself with shepherd's pie, the exercise would do me good.

The evening hadn't gone as I had predicted. I'd thought I might have some trouble convincing Leo to remove the hex, not that I would end up believing he had nothing to do with it. This raised two awkward questions. One: Who had put the hex on Violet? And two: How were we going to get it off?

The evening was cool and crisp, and as I looked up, I saw clouds riding high and the moon playing peekaboo. The lines that Rafe had quoted came into my head. Empress of the night —I hoped she would send some of her lunar power to help us heal Violet.

The moon wasn't full tonight, but it was close. That augured well for magic.

I arrived back at Harrington Street to be overtaken by a car driving way too fast. This was a quiet, residential neighborhood, not the Daytona 500. I turned to glare at the driver and recognized the car. It was Violet's. She screeched to a halt in front of my shop pretty much exactly as I arrived there. She got out of the driver's side. At least I assumed the dark figure wearing a hoodie pulled forward over her face was my cousin. I certainly recognized her passenger. Great-Aunt Lavinia took more time to get out of her side of the car. In the pale light of the moon, I could see the worry on her face.

Seeing me, Violet grabbed my arm. "Unlock the door. Quick."

I thought about what Leo had said about my cousin being barking mad, and the way she was acting now, I understood where he got that idea from.

Still, I did as she asked. She was under a lot of stress right now. No wonder she was acting peculiar. We went in the front door through the shop, but she wouldn't let me turn on a light. She hustled me through the shop and then we went up to my flat through the shop door. As we got to the top of the stairs and into my living area, I was just in time to see the black swish of Nyx's tail disappearing out the living-room window. She'd obviously known who was on the way and wanted nothing to do with a hexed witch. Thanks very much.

I turned on a light, and Violet pulled back her hood.

Even though I'd obviously expected things had gone from bad to worse, I still had to school my face and bite back my cry of combined sympathy and horror. Those big, red pimple things were all over her face now and down her neck, even over the closed eyelid of her bad eye. Her head sported bald patches and, unless she was just feeling insecure, she was getting a hunched back.

"You've got to get this spell off me now!" she cried, as though it were a bat that had flown into her hair.

"I'm trying. I met with Leo tonight. He swears he didn't put the hex on you. And I believed him."

She looked even more distraught now. "What are we going to do?"

Aunt Lavinia spoke now. She wasn't the most fierce of women, except where her granddaughter was concerned. "We will remove the hex. And we will not stop until it's done."

Yeah, that was fine with me.

"But how?"

"I brought my own spell. I haven't used it for years." She paused, and the next words seemed to pain her. "My power is waning. Lucy, you must cast the spell."

"Okay. What do we need?"

I knew I had that soil from the grave of a hanged witch or whatever fake substitute Margaret Twigg had sold me. She'd mentioned black candles, and I had some of those. But what else did we need?

Lavinia held up a cloth bag. "I have everything here."

"Excellent. Shall we cast the spell here and now?"

She gave me an expression that was a bit reminiscent of Margaret Twigg when I had said something that she considered less than intelligent.

"No, Lucy. First, you will need to fetch the skull."

"Right. That makes sense."

"And, powerful as we three are, I'm sorry to say we need Margaret."

Like my evening hadn't already been ruined enough.

North, south, east and west. Earth, air, fire and water. These things always seemed to go in fours. No doubt Margaret Twigg was a capable witch, and the four of us together created some serious magic. But I wasn't sure I wanted to reform this particular quartet. "You do realize it might be Margaret Twigg who made this hex?"

Lavinia stood straighter. "All the more reason for her to help undo the damage she has caused." She shook her finger at me. "And if she has caused this terrible trouble to my granddaughter,

I will begin proceedings to have her removed as the head of our coven."

"You can do that?" It felt weird, like impeaching a president. Not that Margaret Twigg hadn't given cause.

"Perhaps it's time for new blood, anyway." Aunt Lavinia looked at me with a piercing gaze that made me very nervous. Was she suggesting me for the job? I did not want to be that younger blood. I had my hands full, thank you very much, running a knitting shop. Prancing around the standing stones under a full moon chanting once a month was not my idea of a good time. And don't even get me started on the Samhain potluck.

One drama at a time, I reminded myself. "All right. You get hold of Margaret Twigg and tell her we're coming. I'll swing by Rafe's and pick up the skull, and I'll meet you back at Margaret's."

We were all in agreement, and I stopped only to grab my athame, a dagger that was supposed to help separate truth from lies and focus my energy. I had been practicing since I'd been paired with mine not so long ago. If ever anyone needed their truth separated from their lies, it was Margaret Twigg.

I also took the time to throw on a warm blue sweater over my jeans. It comforted me because my grandmother had knit it for me. I called Rafe to let him know what I wanted and told him I was on my way. To my surprise—nay, shock—he stopped me.

"Lucy, stay where you are. I'll get the skull and bring it. I'm driving you to Margaret's place."

"Why? I know I have a bit of trouble with driving on the left-hand side of the road, but I'm perfectly capable."

"It's not that. I don't trust Margaret Twigg. And you have no idea what impact reversing a hex may have on you."

I hadn't thought of that. A creepy feeling came over me. "Are you saying something nasty's going to happen to me?"

I loved my cousin, but I didn't want to end up covered in boils, missing half my hair and a couple of teeth just from trying to do her a good turn.

"No. I have no idea what will happen, but on the off chance there's trouble, I need to be there."

I'd have turned him down if he hadn't used the word need. And if I hadn't seen the bleak despair in his face when he'd thought I'd signed up for a site called Witch Date. So instead of arguing that I was perfectly capable, I said, "Thanks. I'll be ready when you get here."

Now that Violet had left, Nyx poked her nose in the window. I walked over to her and stroked her under her chin the way she liked. "Don't worry. She's gone. It's safe to come in now."

She stepped daintily inside, and I scooped her up, burying my nose in her fur. "What am I going to do about Rafe, Nyx? I'm so confused."

Love is always the answer.

"Now where did that thought come from? Was that you or me?"

Those green-gold eyes blinked at me once.

"You know how to ride a broom. Of course, you know how to put thoughts in my head. But are you sure it's not you who's in love with Rafe?"

I was sure the thought "silly witch" must have come from her.

Now came the second important question. Did I take her with me tonight or didn't I? She was my familiar. But Nyx hated Margaret Twigg probably as violently as whoever put that hex on Violet hated her. Margaret wasn't too fond of Nyx, either, thanks to their history. I didn't want to risk it.

I grabbed my athame and then, prompted by instinct, slipped on a ring that had been my grandmother's. I rarely wore it. It glowed in the face of negative energy. But it had been my grandmother's, and she had worn it every day. Like the sweater, it gave me comfort and reminded me of the connection with the witch who'd passed her power down to me and all the witches in my family who'd gone before me.

WHEN RAFE PULLED UP, I was waiting outside. I had a feeling that time was of the essence.

I got in the sleek, black car, and he accelerated smoothly. "You've got the skull?" I asked him.

"I have."

I don't know why I asked. I could feel the negative energy. And the ring on my finger was pulsing with heat.

"Are you nervous?"

"Why do you ask?"

"I sense it."

Well, then, there wasn't much point in pretending, was there? "I'm sick with nerves. I've got this bad feeling that somehow it's all going to go wrong."

"As it so often does when Margaret Twigg gets involved."

"Aunt Lavinia is furious. She's talking about trying to have Margaret Twigg removed as the head of our coven if it turns out she had anything to do with this hex."

He turned to me. "Like a palace coup."

"Exactly like that."

"Who's the usurper in waiting? Not your great-aunt Lavinia, surely. She's rather old."

"I don't think it's herself that Aunt Lavinia has in mind." Something in my tone caught his attention.

"You don't mean she wants to put you at the head of the coven?"

I didn't remotely want the job, but I was offended that he

clearly thought I wasn't up to the task. I sounded a bit huffy when I said, "What's wrong with that?"

He turned to stare at me. "What's wrong with that? Is that a serious question? Everything's wrong with it. You have mighty powers, but you're young and untried. You're not properly trained. Margaret Twigg has many faults, but she can see the inevitable. You will be the head of the coven one day. But she's right when she pushes you to learn everything you can. You're not ready."

Every word of what he said was true. Unfortunately. Though I wondered how he knew so much about witch business. "Rafe, I don't want the job now, and I'm never going to want the job."

"I think it's a bit like being king. Queen in your case. One doesn't have a choice. One must bow to destiny."

"Sometimes destiny sucks."

He laughed softly. "That it does."

CHAPTER 14

We pulled up behind Violet's car in the long, pea-gravel drive leading up to Margaret's cottage. There were no electric lights on in the house, but the flickering of candlelight made the stone cottage even more secretive and eerie.

We both got out of the car. He retrieved a burlap bag that had a skull-shaped lump in it. Before he handed it to me, he said, "Be careful. One cry, and I'll be there. You know it."

And I did. At the first sign of trouble, he'd be at my side. Before he handed me the skull, he leaned down and kissed me.

Love is always the answer. Sounded like something you'd read on a greeting card. And yet, sometimes the most simple messages were both the most powerful and the most true.

I clung to him for a minute before pulling away and taking the skull. Gran's ring nearly burned my finger as I carried the cursed skull to the cottage.

I didn't even have to knock on the door. It opened before I raised my hand. Margaret Twigg looked particularly dramatic tonight. Bathed in candlelight, she wore a long, black robe with a bright pink scarf and pink jeweled earrings and necklace. Her crazy, corkscrew curls seemed to be having a party on the top of her head. Her lipstick was a vivid slash of a matching pink, and her eyes gleamed with wicked excitement. She was looking forward to this ceremony.

Then her mouth turned down. "Is that it?"

I offered her the bag. "Yes."

She held her hands up. "I don't want to touch it. Bring it into the front room."

The front room? I'd only ever been in her kitchen and the shed where she kept herbs and some of the more noxious of the substances she used in her spells and potions. Perhaps a dead body or two.

I walked in to find a surprisingly comfortable and almost traditional-looking living room. What the British insisted on calling a lounge or drawing room if they were fancy. A wood fire was crackling in the grate, adding its light to the candles that burned. All of them black. Violet stood staring into the fire, looking wretched. The firelight reflected off her pimples or boils, whatever they were, making them look even more painful.

My great-aunt Lavinia was staring at a sculpture on a side table. It was a squat, naked and very pregnant woman. No doubt it was some kind of fertility goddess.

It was obvious that Great-Aunt Lavinia had already unpacked her bag. It lay empty on the scarred, oak coffee table that had been pushed towards a comfortable-looking couch upholstered in purple fabric. A chunky woolen throw hanging over the back of the sofa looked hand-knit. I didn't think Margaret Twigg was a knitter. Somebody must have given it to her as a gift. Or in payment for something.

Knitting made me think of my vampires, and once more the idea skittered across my mind that Sylvia was the one behind the hex and that it had been intended for me. But why would she barter a hand-knit throw for a hex? She'd just buy it.

Besides, if she was knitting a garment, it would have turned out a lot better than this one.

In the middle of the room was a circle of black candles waiting to be lit. None of the three of us seemed to know what to say, and so it was quiet until Margaret joined us. I was still holding the skull. I didn't know where to put it or what to do with it. It was like arriving at a birthday party with entirely the wrong gift.

Then Margaret came in. She looked at me sharply. "Did you bring the earth from the grave of a hanged witch?" she asked me. I knew she had a jar full of that stuff. I couldn't believe she was making me use the tiny bit she'd overcharged me for. But luckily, again knowing Margaret Twigg, I had it in my bag. I brought it out and handed it to her.

Something caught the light on the floor inside the circle of unlit candles, and I realized there was a mirror there.

I said, "Do I put the skull on top of the mirror?" It seemed like an obvious thing to do, given the way these spells worked. Reflecting the hex back to where it came from was best done with a mirror.

She shook her head. "Not yet. Take it out of the bag and step inside the circle."

I did as instructed. Touching the skull made my whole body twitch with dread. I put my handbag on the floor outside the circle and reached in for my athame. My dagger caught the light a little bit the way the mirror had and glowed. I was glad I'd brought the dagger with me, even if we didn't need it. As the ring had, the athame made me feel more powerful and connected.

Seeing it, Margaret Twigg nodded in rare approval. "Good. You've some sense then."

Since I had no idea what to reply, I didn't bother. The skull was slightly rough beneath my fingers. I hated touching the thing. The ring that reacted to bad energy was so warm, it was nearly burning my finger. Mind you, that could be from Margaret Twigg.

I stepped inside the circle, and she directed the other two to do the same. She came in last, bringing a tall, thick, black pillar candle. She glanced around at the three of us. "You definitely don't know who put the hex on you?"

Aunt Lavinia answered, "No. Do you?"

I sort of moved my knife, trying to look casual, though the point that was supposed to separate truth from lies ended up pointing directly at Margaret Twigg.

She answered, "No. I don't believe this is one of mine."

The knife didn't give me any feedback. Maybe she was telling the truth. And then again, maybe she wasn't.

She inspected the skull, though she still refused to touch it. She made me turn it this way and that as she studied the object.

Violet groaned a few times, and I could see the hunch in her back growing more pronounced. This had better work, and fast.

Finally, Margaret spoke. "Lucy, take the words that are written backwards on the skull and use your dagger to carve them into this candle."

"You want me to write a backwards message in a candle?"

She shook her head, impatient once again. Her curls seemed like so many fingers scolding me. "No. We reverse everything. You'll write it as we would read it."

Okay. It wasn't that hard, but I still felt their gazes on me as I awkwardly carved each letter into the wax of the candle. It took a while to carve the letters in wax, especially the g and d. I struggled with the curves.

It looked like a kid's early attempt at printing, but the words were legible enough. "Grow ugly, wither and die."

It was horrible to carve such a cruel message. Even though I was trying to remove the curse, I felt like I was casting one.

"Now, light the candles."

She didn't offer me a match. She looked at me with challenge in her eyes. Oh, I could light candles. Just to be fancy, I used my knife. I waved it slowly around the circle, and each wick sprang to life obediently. Naturally, I didn't get a compliment from Margaret Twigg, but I didn't get some sarcastic insult either. I called that a win. And then she directed me to sprinkle the earth of the hanged witch around the edge of the mirror. And now, finally, I could put the skull down. I leaned forward to do so, more than happy to get rid of the nasty thing, but she stopped me.

"Violet? Break the mirror."

I supposed I should have seen this coming.

Violet stepped forward and stomped on the mirror with violent force and a howl of anger. It cracked in about five places. "Now prick your finger with a shard of mirror." I could hardly stand to watch. Like Violet didn't have enough hurts already.

When that was done, Margaret nodded to me. "Now you may put the skull down on top of the broken mirror and set the candle beside it."

I did as I was instructed. I was starting to get gooseflesh now, more so when Violet dripped blood onto the skull. The four of us together had undeniable power. And perhaps there was a reason the cottage was situated this way, because as the moon rose, its light hit the broken mirror. Instead of joining hands, the four of us focused our hands toward the skull, and Margaret intoned,

> Spirits of the north, south, east and west,
> we call on you to put wrong right.
> Let the person who has inflicted this curse
> find it reflected back to them but even worse.
> Take away this hurt and harm
> and send it back from whence it came.

*Moon is for fire, blood is for water, graveyard for earth, and
spirits for air.*
We conjure you to do our bidding,
As we will, so mote it be.

I felt a sudden compulsion come over me. There was such
power in my arm and hand. My grandmother's ring was hot and
glowing, and my athame looked like it was on fire. I'd never seen
it like that before.

As I pointed my glowing dagger at the skull, there was a
crack and a tiny explosion, and then the skull seemed to
implode upon itself, crumbling to dust.

Margaret wasn't one to give out compliments like they were
candy. When she said in a quiet, dry tone, "You did well," I felt
like I got an A+ in class.

But had our attempt to reverse the hex worked?

I looked at Violet. We all looked at Violet. Was she standing
straighter? I thought she was. She didn't say anything though. In
fact, she was starting to sway.

"Violet? Are you o—"

She crumpled. She'd have hit the floor if I hadn't gotten
there in time. She keeled over on me, and not knowing what else
to do with her, I sank down, taking her with me until I could lay
her on the floor. I was quite alarmed. So was Great-Aunt Lavinia.
She looked at Margaret.

"Is my granddaughter all right?"

"She will be."

Still, Aunt Lavinia got to her knees and placed her hand on
her granddaughter's forehead.

"She's hot. Like she has a fever."

"That's good. She's got to get the poison out of her."

The clouds must have moved or the moon shifted its position, but suddenly Violet's face was bathed in moonlight. There

were a few scabs on her face, but the awful boils were gone. Even though both eyes were closed, the swelling was going down on her bad eye.

We stayed with her until she woke, looking a little like Snow White minus the handsome prince. She put a shaky hand to her head. "What happened?" She glanced around at us. "I feel so strange."

Then she seemed to remember everything that had occurred. She put her hands to her face. "A mirror. I must have a mirror."

I went to take one of the broken pieces, and Margaret smacked my hand. "Not that one."

Instead, she went to a table and opened a drawer. She brought over an ornate-looking hand mirror that no doubt did double duty as a scrying mirror and handed it to Violet. For some reason, none of us turned on an electric light. We simply moved candles closer. But even in candlelight, it was pretty clear that she was almost back to normal. Her hair was once more thick and lustrous. Even the dyed streak was exactly where it had been before. In the couple of minutes it took for her to gaze at herself in wonder, the last scabs disappeared. Last of all, she smiled. To my great relief, there was no gap of a missing tooth. She was as good as new.

Since I had opened the circle, it was my job to close it and extinguish the lights. I'd never been so happy to do that.

I looked at the pile of goat skull dust sitting on top of the broken mirror and said to Margaret Twigg, "What do we do with that?" I wanted to bury it far, far away, under a heavy stone.

She gave me one of her wicked smiles. "I'll find a use for it."

I'd bet she would too. I didn't ask.

"I'm so tired," Violet said. "I need to go to bed."

That broke up the evening, which was just as well, because I don't think any of us wanted to sit around in Margaret's living room socializing. She seemed as happy to get rid of us as we were to leave.

"Blessed be," she said as we were leaving, and we returned the salutation.

Outside, Violet suddenly hugged me tightly. "Thank you, Lucy."

"I didn't do anything."

"I don't care. Thank you anyway."

Even Great-Aunt Lavinia hugged me. I watched them into their car and then walked over to the black car, where Rafe was quietly waiting. I got in and heard classical music playing softly. He looked at me searchingly.

"You survived the ordeal, then?"

Adrenaline was surging through my body. I felt like a kick-ass heroine. "More than survived. I feel powerful. Awesome. We did it, Rafe. It was so cool."

While he drove, I told him about the whole evening. Violet might be exhausted, but I was wired. "And my dagger glowed with power. I really need to learn more. I'm going to take my witch lessons more seriously from now on."

Once we were heading back, he said, "Do you fancy a night-cap? Or shall I take you straight home?"

His place was much closer than mine. And I was so wired, I didn't want to be alone. Besides, I wanted to be with him.

"Your place."

Rafe wasn't big on showy emotions. He reached over and took my hand.

CHAPTER 15

I wasn't a bit surprised when Violet called me the next morning to say she couldn't possibly come to work. She was still traumatized from the experience of having been hexed and terribly worried that all her hair hadn't come back yet. Knowing Violet, I imagined she'd already spent some anxious hours in front of the mirror. I didn't blame her. I'd probably have done the same thing. I assured her that I thought her hair had looked full and healthy even last night but told her to take her time coming back.

I could always get extra help in the shop if I needed it. Mabel and Clara were only too happy to help, and even Hester could sometimes be relied on. I also had a couple of local university students who worked for me when they needed extra cash. However, I wasn't sure I needed the help. I'd play it by ear. And so I opened as I usually did. Though I had added one extra step to my morning opening routine. I checked outside the front door that there was nothing magical cluttering the entrance to the shop. I was pleased to see there wasn't but still took fifteen minutes before opening time to do a smudging ritual to get rid of the negative energy that was still hanging

116

around, not only from the hex object itself but from Violet's reaction to it.

While I was waving a smoking stick of sage and chanting, Nyx was doing her morning rounds. When both of us were satisfied there was neither mouse nor bad energy in Cardinal Woolsey's, we got on with our day. Me, to restock the shelves. Nyx for her morning nap.

I felt so much lighter today. Not only because I'd cleansed my workspace but knowing that Violet was back to normal. I did spend a minute or two wondering who was on the other end of the hex and if they'd experienced any bad effects from it. Hopefully, reversing a curse when you didn't know who'd put it on you was like marking an envelope "Return to Sender" that had no return address on it. I liked the idea that the hex was wandering aimlessly around in the atmosphere and would soon die, like a parasite without a host to support it.

I did brisk business that morning, and surprisingly, or not surprisingly given the circumstances, everybody was in a buying mood. Customers weren't leaving Cardinal Woolsey's as quickly as they could. Today, it was as though the opposite had happened. As though I had some magic spell drawing them in. I would never do such a thing, even if I did know a spell like that. It would be cheating. For me, half the fun was seeing how I could grow the business using my burgeoning skills as a digital marketer. I'd followed my grandmother's tradition of selling high-quality wools, and wherever possible, I sourced them from the British Isles. I highlighted that fact in all my marketing.

By the afternoon, I knew my sales were way up over a typical day. I was thrilled.

When Felicity Stevens and Jemima Taft walked in, I wasn't even surprised, though I was gratified to see them. I had assumed all that talk about Jemima taking up knitting was just the slightly inebriated conversation of someone who might think it was a great idea to take up knitting after drinking a bottle of wine and then woke up the next morning to realize it was a terrible idea.

If they even remembered the conversation.

The fact that she was here suggested the opposite.

Felicity Stevens came towards me as though we were the best of friends. "Lucy. I've had the best idea."

"What is it?"

"Jemima and I were just passing, and we thought it would be fun to get together tonight for a girls' night."

I felt so flattered. I had friends in Oxford, sure. But they tended to be either undead or of the witch variety. With regular mortals, I struggled a bit. I was friendly with Alice, who worked across the street in Frogg's Books. But since she'd married Charlie, the owner of the shop, she didn't have as much time as she once had.

To have non-magical women around my age seeking me out for friendship was kind of a thrill and felt like part of the great trajectory this day was already on.

"Absolutely," I said, sounding as pleased as I felt. "I'd love to."

They shared an almost conspiratorial grin. "I told you she'd say yes," Felicity said.

Jemima spoke up now. "The thing is, I've got a business dinner I have to attend first. Why don't I meet you both in the front lobby bar of the Wainwright Hotel?"

My eyebrows rose of their own accord. The Wainwright Hotel was a long way from The Flag and Bear. It was one of the best hotels in Oxford and catered to a very high-end clientele. I imagined the drink prices in the lobby bar would be eye-wateringly high. However, I consoled myself that I rarely went out. I could afford to splurge now and then.

She continued, "It's a bore, I know. But if we meet there, then we can head out somewhere more interesting after that."

That sounded fine to me, and so I agreed that I would meet Felicity at seven in the lobby, and then about eight o'clock, when her dinner was finished, Jemima would come and find us.

I closed up shop at five as usual, fed Nyx, decided I hadn't been eating enough greens so made myself a very healthy salad with a piece of grilled salmon on it. Having polished that off, I discovered I was still hungry and dug into my grandmother's ginger snaps, which she kept me supplied with in the special cookie tin she'd had ever since I could remember.

It was weird to feel nostalgic about someone who was still in existence, but there was no mistaking the fact that my relationship with my grandmother was very different. We couldn't sit around together over cookies and tea the way we used to. Still, I was glad I still had her in my life. Even if it was weird to see her sleek and strong, no longer needing her glasses, and since Sylvia had gotten hold of her, she bought expensive clothes and always had hair and makeup impeccably done. I finished up my cookies, tidied the kitchen and brushed my teeth.

Then came the dilemma.

The perennial dilemma of every woman I knew. What to wear?

My wardrobe, understandably, was filled with knitted items, none of which I'd actually knitted myself. I had a couple of dresses suitable for fancier occasions but nothing that said Wainwright Hotel.

I glanced at my watch. If I'd had time, I'd have run up to the shopping center. With a couple of days' notice, I'd have gone to London to shop. However, I didn't have time to buy a new outfit and get to the Wainwright in an hour. Anyway, this wasn't a job interview or my wedding. It was three women getting together for drinks. They'd seen me in my hand-knitted jumpers and jeans. They must know I wasn't a fashion plate.

In the end, I settled on a beautiful midnight-blue sweater that Sylvia had knitted me. I hadn't worn anything Sylvia had knitted for me in some time, but it was time to get over myself. With it, I wore a very tasteful diamond necklace she had bought me. Just putting those clothes on made me soften my feelings towards the glamorous vamp. She was who she was. I hadn't died, no thanks to her, but maybe it was time to forgive. I had a pair of black silk trousers that went with the sweater, and I put on the best black shoes that I had. No one was going to confuse me with the very posh Jemima, but they weren't going to throw me out on the street either.

I let my hair hang in loose curls, went heavier on makeup than usual, and called myself done.

Since I'd be drinking, I called a cab to take me to the inn, which was on the edge of town.

The car dropped me off a couple of minutes before seven. A uniformed bellhop greeted me and rushed ahead of me to open the door, and I walked into hush and splendor.

I'd never been inside. Originally a Tudor coaching inn, the Wainwright had kept the best of the old inn—the massive fireplaces, dark wooden beams and the old windows—but added all the luxuries of the present time.

I looked around for a couple of minutes, getting my bearings and then saw the lobby bar discreetly off to the side. It looked to be an anteroom for a fancy dining room. No doubt that's where Jemima was at the moment. A lot of her business seemed to involve wining and dining her very important and wealthy clients.

Felicity was already there. She was concentrating on her phone. A bottle of champagne sat cooling in a bucket beside her, and a tray with three glasses sat on the round table in front of her. I walked up and said, "Are we celebrating?"

She glanced up, again looking delighted to see me. Her eyes were sparkling as though she were looking forward to something really fantastic. "It's from Jemima. She told us to get started and she'll join us as soon as she can."

"That's generous of her," I said, now able to glimpse the label. I might not be a champagne expert, but I knew that vintage Dom Perignon did not come off the wine shelf in Tesco.

Felicity didn't even signal before a uniformed server appeared at her elbow. "Shall I open the champagne, madam? Or are we waiting for a third?"

"Go ahead and open it now."

The bottle made a very discreet pop. There were no flying champagne corks and foaming bottles in this establishment. He poured us two glasses and returned the champagne to its bucket and, with a small bow, disappeared as silently as he'd appeared.

Felicity held up the flute of bubbling, straw-gold liquid and tapped my glass with it.

"To new friendships."

"To new friendships," I echoed. I don't know why, but something about her excitement was making me uneasy. I mean, I was a nice person, and who wouldn't want to be friends with me? But her suppressed excitement seemed a bit over the top.

Still, I was the first to admit it had been a while since I'd been able to let loose and enjoy a night with normal, female friends. I was probably imagining things. I sipped the champagne and found it as delightful as I'd imagined it would be.

"Tell me about yourself," she said, leaning forward.

That's one of those questions that always leaves me tongue-tied. The most interesting parts of my life, I couldn't talk about, and nobody wanted to hear me ramble on about wool and customers. I stuck to a skimpy autobiography. How I'd grown up in Boston and when my beloved grandmother had died, she'd left Cardinal Woolsey's to me.

"That was nice of her. That property must be worth a few quid. I wish someone would leave me a prime bit of property in Oxford."

I smiled politely. My fingers were beginning to tingle with some kind of witch's intuition. Never a good sign. "Your turn," I said cheerfully. "Tell me about yourself."

I'd barely drunk half my glass of champagne, and I saw her signal the waiter to come over and top our glasses. Was she planning to get me drunk? Why would she? Again, I doubted my suspicions. But I couldn't get away from the instinct that something odd was going on here.

CHAPTER 16

"My life hasn't been easy, Lucy," she said, looking very sorry for herself. "Daddy and Mummy ran through the family money, you see, so I've had to make my own way. Not like so many of my school friends." She cast an almost furtive glance toward the dining room, where even now her best friend, Jemima, was at a business dinner. If she was implying that Jemima had it easy, I'd seen no evidence of that. Jemima looked like a card-carrying workaholic to me.

"After school, I got a job in the Peter Bedworth Gallery here in Oxford. Peter's an old friend of Daddy's from Eton. Comes from old money. He'll be a baronet one day. He studied fine art and then set up a gallery." Her face twisted as though she were about to sneeze. "He employs young women who've been to the right schools, like Salisbury Ladies' College, where Jemima and I met. People like us can get the right prospects to pay an arm and a leg for a painting."

"That's quite a way to do business."

"Was, darling. I got the sack," she said.

"Really?"

I wasn't all that interested, but I could tell she was enjoying sharing her supposed hard-knock life. "After his divorce, Peter wasn't the same." She held her hands up and wiggled her fingers, nearly slopping champagne in the process. "Got very handsy."

I nodded.

"I helped bring in a Paul Klee, and we got top price. Peter wanted to celebrate, just the two of us, if you know what I mean."

Of course I did. I hated these kinds of stories. Powerful older men abusing their authority over much younger women. "He made a pass at you."

"And when I slapped his face, he was furious. He didn't say anything, but a few days later, he telephoned me at home to tell me not to bother coming in anymore."

"But that's illegal, surely?"

She shrugged. "I went to a solicitor, but since he paid me a reasonable sum, there wasn't anything I could do. So you find me temporarily jobless."

"I'm so sorry. I'm sure you'll find something."

She waved a hand as though conducting a choir. "Oh, I'm sure I'll come out all right. I have plans."

I had a sneaking suspicion that her latest scheme involved William.

The bottle was growing low, and I tried to go easy. I wasn't a big drinker, and the champagne was getting to me a little bit. It seemed to be hitting Felicity harder, though. She was getting quite flushed in the face.

Finally, she leaned in. "I'm so pleased we've got this time alone together. I feel I can trust you, Lucy. I've absolutely fallen for William Thresher. Tell me what I have to do to show him I care?"

Now the penny dropped. Or I should say the millions of pounds dropped. Every conversation I could recall with Felicity had ended up about money or property or her wishing she had more. I didn't grudge her wanting to marry rich. Loads of people did. But I definitely grudged her William. I tried to give her the benefit of the doubt, but somebody with dollar signs in their eyes was not going to be the right wife for him.

I thought my best bet was to head her off gently. "William's an amazing butler. He's made a profession out of something that few people care about anymore. Plus, he cooks like a dream. You've tasted his cooking."

"Yes, yes. But, surely, once he settles down, he won't want to be a servant anymore."

And there it was. That snobbery that I knew and did not love.

"I don't think William sees it as servitude. He sees his role as a career." I gave her a smile as fake as her own. "And anyone who settles with William is going to have to be okay with that."

This wasn't the answer she wanted. "And what's his wife supposed to do while he's polishing the silver and delivering messages to his lordship? Scrub the fireplaces?"

"I suppose that would be up to William's wife."

"Well, you're rather cozy with his employer. Couldn't you hint to him that he should start looking for another butler?"

"I wouldn't dare. Those two have a bond. He'll never find anyone who manages his estate better, and William is happy."

"But William doesn't need to work."

I was furious. Coldly furious. I knew darn well that William hadn't told her about his circumstances. I suspected she'd pumped her financial advisor friend as ruthlessly as she was trying to pump me.

"I wouldn't know," I said. Technically that was true. Rafe had refused to tell me any details about William's financial position, but I wasn't a fool. It was pretty clear the Thresher family had been well provided for throughout the years.

I wasn't sure how the conversation would have turned from there, but the awkward moment was saved when Jemima Taft walked out of the dining room. With her was Nico, the man I'd seen her with earlier, and another man I didn't know. She looked cool, impeccable, and stone-cold sober.

She paused as though surprised to see us and said, "Hello. How nice to see you both."

Nico followed her gaze, and his eyes narrowed slightly when they rested on my face as I saw him trying to place me. Then he came forward, looking both charming and somewhat wolfish. "Your advice was excellent. The meal your friend William prepared us was magnifico." And he made a starburst motion with his hand. So very Italian.

I felt as flattered, by proxy, as though I'd had anything to do with the dinner. "I'm glad. William really is an artist in the kitchen."

Then he nodded to Felicity. "Evening."

"Good evening." Felicity looked delighted to see him. "Won't you join us?"

So much for girls' night out. But it made sense. If Nico had been at Jemima's dinner, he must be rich too. I was glad to see Felicity spreading her net wide. She'd need to, as I was going to do everything I could to make sure William swam out of her reach.

He shook his head. "Thank you, no. I have an errand to run."

He turned and kissed Jemima on both cheeks. "*Ciao, Bella.* I will call you tomorrow."

The other man came forward now. He was blond and slightly built. "Sergei," Felicity cried as though it was a special treat to see him.

"Good to see you again," he said in a slight Russian accent. Now he too kissed Jemima on both cheeks, and then the two men walked all the way out of the hotel, talking in low tones.

Jemima waited until they had left and then sank into the third chair.

"Phew," she said. "That was dull. I need a drink."

She hadn't even finished the words and our same server was back pouring her a glass and filling ours. "Another bottle, if you please," she said to him.

"My pleasure, madam."

She glanced between us. "Do you mind if we just stay here? I haven't the energy to go somewhere else."

We both agreed that was fine.

To the server, she said, "And bring some snacks."

I was shocked. "Didn't you just eat dinner?"

She looked sad. "One never does at these dos. I have to keep my wits about me. I'm concentrating so hard, you see. I daren't touch a sip of alcohol or eat more than a nibble of food or I'm distracted."

That aligned with what Violet had said.

The evening got a lot better after that. Jemima Taft downed champagne as though it was water, and as she relaxed, she grew more talkative. She was amusing in a wicked, sarcastic way. She knew gossip about celebrities that never showed up in *Tattler* or *Hello*. And when she recounted an amusing incident at one of those horse races where fancy hats were required, she didn't sound like she was boasting. It was just the way she lived.

Felicity joined in as though she lived in that world, too, but she still reminded me of the knockoff bag when set against the real thing. She was almost like the original but never quite.

Still, they were good company, and I decided to put the grilling I'd gotten from Felicity to bad manners. And she had helped me with one thing. I'd tried to keep an open mind about her relationship with William. Now, I was full on against it. I hoped William wasn't in love with her. I doubted he was. No doubt he was just flattered that somebody was showing him so much attention. I hoped so, anyway. Because if he did get serious, I suspected he was going to get his heart broken.

"Nico seems interesting. Are you seeing him?" I asked.

"I never date clients. It would be completely inappropriate."

"How did he make his money?" I had a hard time understanding how people who didn't have hundreds of years to grow their stash managed to get so rich. "Or is it family money?"

She giggled. "You could say that." She leaned in. "Crime family. I don't ask where the money comes from. In my business, best not. So long as it comes in clean and passes money-laundering laws, I've fulfilled my obligation." She lowered her voice. "But there are rumors." Then she put her hand over her mouth. "But you did not hear that. Completely confidential."

She excused herself for the washroom, and Felicity leaned in, her breath boozy. "She's the most professional woman at the office. Absolutely top notch. But get her loaded, and she spills the goods. Such fun."

"It's nice she has a friend she can trust."

Felicity nodded. "She does try to introduce me to interesting men. I went to the right schools, can fit in with that world, but I'm poor as a church mouse. She thought I might fancy Nico or Sergei." She glanced at me slyly. "But William was so much more interesting."

Every instinct in my witch's body told me Jemima Taft had told her friend that William had a lot more to offer than his talent in the kitchen.

We nibbled on snacks and downed more champagne. At some point, we got out our phones and snapped photos. Felicity suddenly said, "What's this hush-hush deal then? You can tell us."

Jemima was pretty far gone by this time. She'd drunk the better part of two bottles of champagne, I was certain. I didn't know where she was putting it all.

Instead of telling her friend to mind her own business, she leaned in and told us in a low voice that Hurst and Havers, tailors to royalty, who'd been a private company for a couple of hundred years, was vulnerable to a takeover.

For this, she had a top-secret dinner? Buying a tailor didn't seem that exciting to me.

Felicity, however, looked aghast. "Hurst and Havers is for sale?"

"Keep your voice down. No. It isn't. But Nico says its balance sheet is weak and he's planning a takeover. He's got a friend on the board who's willing to help."

"What's so exciting about buying a tailor?" I asked.

"Shh. Keep your voice down. If anyone got wind of this deal, the whole thing could blow up. These things require absolute finesse and complete discretion."

I was still confused.

"It's the brand, Lucy. You wouldn't understand, being American. It's utterly exclusive. Imagine it as a global brand? With the right financing, it could be huge. Huge."

Felicity looked suitably impressed.

I excused myself to go to the washroom, and as I stepped into the lobby, I nearly crossed paths with Nico on his way to the elevator. I slowed my steps so he wouldn't see me. I didn't feel like chatting to the charming but possibly criminal Nico. He must be staying at the hotel.

When I got back to the table, a new bottle of champagne cooled in the bucket, and my glass was once more full.

"Lucy," Jemima said grandly. "You must tell us all about Rafe Crosyer. I understand you're friends. He's very tall, dark and mysterious, isn't he?"

"He is."

Who knows what would have happened next, but Felicity burst in, "Yes, but he can't keep William as his butler. It's positively medieval. William has rights." The champagne had caught up and was pretty much overtaking her. She was having trouble focusing. She began to scratch at her chest. "I'm so itchy."

It was close to midnight, and we were all the worse for wear. "I have to go," I said. "Got to get up in the morning."

Jemima glanced at her watch and gasped. "Yes. So do I. We're putting the final financing deal together tomorrow. It's going to be a big day."

As we left the hotel, a black Mercedes pulled up. "Let us drop you somewhere," Jemima said.

It saved me having to get a cab, and she'd begun a story about someone I would never be able to respect again when I saw them on the television. So I agreed.

She turned around. "Come on, Felicity, I've got to get up in the morning," she said. I turned around, and Felicity was heading unsteadily towards us.

"I've broken a heel on my new shoe. It just snapped off," she complained. "They cost a fortune, too."

"Never mind. You can buy some new ones. Just get in."

"Oh, give me a minute. It's so hot."

It wasn't hot. It was cold. I was shivering inside my coat, but her cheeks were bright red. I'd assumed she was one of those people that got flushed cheeks when they drank alcohol. But maybe she was coming down with something.

Jemima obviously thought the same thing. "You're not getting sick, are you? I can't have that. I've got a busy week coming up."

"No. I'm just itchy."

She began to unbutton her blouse. Jemima and I together pushed her into the car and climbed in with her. "Home, please," she said to the driver. "If you don't mind, we'll head to my place first. Felicity usually stays over when we've had a night out. She lives outside of town, and it saves her the drive. Or, in this case, an expensive cab ride."

"No, that's fine." I was curious to see where she lived.

By this time Felicity had pulled open her blouse. I drew in a sharp breath as we drove under a street light and she was brightly illuminated. Her chest was covered in scales.

"You've got some kind of rash," I said.

"No wonder I'm so itchy." She went to scratch her chest, and I noticed her fingers were curling over like claws. I didn't say anything. I was getting a very bad feeling about this.

If her hair started falling out or her teeth did, I was going to have a pretty good idea what was wrong.

THE TOWN CAR pulled up in front of a lovely Victorian townhouse on Kingston Road.

Even though I was curious to see where Jemima lived, I was much more concerned about Felicity's state of health. The driver got out. He was a solid man in his fifties with a round face and thick black eyebrows that met over his nose.

"Oh, Dick, what would I do without you?" Jemima asked, as he, along with me and Jemima, helped Felicity out of the back. Once we had her on the sidewalk, she swayed until Jemima held onto her.

"Do you think she should see a doctor?" I asked.

Jemima said, "No, she'll be fine. It's just a rash."

I didn't think Felicity was fine. She was pretty wasted, or I might have tackled her then and there about the hex. But neither of them were in any condition for sensible conversation. And, in fairness, I was in no condition to question them.

The best thing for all of us would be a good night's sleep. I had Felicity's mobile number because we were apparently now

BFFs. I'd call her in the morning. I told her that was my plan and then said goodnight to them both.

I stood on the sidewalk and watched them as they opened the gate and walked into a small front garden behind a hedge and then on a path to the door. It looked to me like Felicity was dragging her back foot. Uh-oh. This was not good.

After they were inside, Dick, the driver, and I returned to our previous positions in the Mercedes. I gave my address, and we slipped smoothly back into the night. It wasn't more than five minutes by car to my place, but I didn't feel like walking, especially not so late at night.

Dick said, "Don't worry about them. I can't tell you the number of times that I've dropped them off in a worse state than that. They'll be back at it tomorrow. Amazing constitutions, the pair of them."

"You drive them regularly?"

"Oh, yes. Jemima's a regular customer of the limousine service I work for. She always asks for me." His big shoulders moved up and down. "She knows I'll look out for her, and the way she drinks, she needs someone to make sure she gets home all right."

"She does this often, then?" She must have a constitution of iron; he was right.

Instead of answering directly, he said, "She's got a high-stress job. Likes to let loose when she can. And who can blame her? Felicity's what you might call her wingman. Not to worry."

But I was worried. If I was right, Felicity had been so determined to bag William that she'd bought a hex to use against Violet, presumably seeing her as competition. She'd need more than a strong constitution to withstand the effects of the now-reversed hex.

I was going to have to speak to Margaret Twigg and see what the options were for helping Felicity. I hoped that she could get the witch who'd sold her the hex to remove it. That seemed simplest, but I was very fuzzy on the procedure. Once a curse had been reversed, could its originator still remove it? Or would that be a job for me, Violet, Margaret, and Aunt Lavinia? Having reversed the hex, were we now the ones who could remove it?

There was one more possibility that I refused to consider.

What if no one could now remove the hex?

CHAPTER 17

*T*he car dropped me off, and Dick gave me his card, telling me to call him if I ever needed driving anywhere. I thanked him, and he kindly waited until I was inside.

Then, I pretty much fell into bed. When I woke up, I felt as though I'd stuffed half the stock of Cardinal Woolsey's into my mouth and chewed on it all night. Apart from a dry, woolly mouth, I also had a headache.

I thought I'd taken it pretty easy last night, and compared with my two companions, I'd been the model of discretion. Practically a teetotaler, and still I had a massive headache and felt very queasy. It would be a long time before I could face champagne again.

The other two must feel like hell this morning. Or maybe they drank like this so often they were used to it and no longer suffered.

I picked up my phone and contemplated calling Felicity to see how she was feeling this morning, but it was only eight o'clock. Besides, I needed to get myself together before I could even think straight, never mind talk sense to another human.

Maybe Felicity and Jemima could party all night and still go to work the next day as though nothing had happened. I, on the other hand, urgently needed a couple of aspirin, a strong cup of coffee and a gallon of water.

While I brewed coffee, I pondered the events of the night before, especially the end of the evening, when Felicity had developed some disturbing symptoms. A bizarre disease or allergy? Or was it the hex? In my fuddled condition last night, I'd jumped to the hex conclusion, but in the cold light of day, that seemed absurd. Felicity Stevens put a hex on Violet that would curse her to *Grow ugly, wither and die?* Surely a person saved that kind of nastiness for their worst enemy.

She'd barely even met my cousin. Why would she hate her enough to want evil things to happen to her? For a guy? For William? Had Felicity really nosed out the attraction between Violet and William, as I had? And as it seemed, Rafe had? It seemed obvious to me, but I knew Violet well, and Rafe obviously knew William pretty well. But Felicity didn't know either of them.

If Felicity Stevens had bought the hex—and it was a big if— she must have been incredibly sensitive to any possible rival for William's affections and extremely determined to get rid of them. I thought back to those moments when I had really found Felicity not very likable. Mainly they were when she acted like money was all that mattered. When she'd talked about how William had too much money to stay on as Rafe's butler, especially when he got married, she hadn't been speaking hypothetically. She'd been thinking about herself as the next Mrs. Thresher, and it was pretty clear she didn't fancy a life tucked away at Crosyer Manor making Rafe's life run smoothly. She also very clearly didn't want any competition on her path to the altar.

William was decent enough and thought little enough of

his own attractiveness that a determined woman might be able to fool him. And Felicity Stevens was nothing if not determined.

I wondered if marrying well had become an obsession. For it wasn't only William she seemed to like. When Nico had emerged from dinner with Jemima, Felicity had fluttered her eyelashes at him and invited him to join us. And never mind we were on a girls' night out.

As I popped toast in the toaster, I wondered what it must be like for her to always be second best to her closest friend. Not to be able to shop at the top-end designer shops but to make do with the second string. Felicity struck me as a woman who did not want to be second string in anything. She wanted what her friend had, and I suspected she wanted it very badly. As I continued my train of thought, it became less of a stretch to imagine her putting a hex on a rival. But why not just something to make Violet less attractive to men or William in particular? Why go the extra length? Why curse someone with a lingering death? That was beyond self-interest. That was just plain vicious.

However, she'd got tangled up in dark witchcraft somehow. I could imagine how easy it would be to request a fairly mild hex and find yourself purchasing something much more dramatic. Anyone who'd sell that kind of black magic wouldn't be concerned about health and safety.

A cold shiver went down my spine as I thought not only how much of a near miss Violet had had but how, when reversing the curse, we'd thrown some pretty hefty dark magic back on Felicity Stevens.

Margaret Twigg would argue that she'd brought trouble on herself. She'd tried to beat her competition back with a very big stick. Now it was her rival who'd wielded the stick back at her, only first she'd given it a heftier wallop. The only question was, how hefty? I glanced at the kitchen clock and knew I had to get moving if I was going to open the shop on time.

Now that I had some food in my stomach and coffee in my system and the aspirin was doing its job, my headache began to lift. I still wasn't feeling in top form, but I could function. I was just brushing my teeth and thinking about heading downstairs when my mobile rang.

My first thought was that it might be Felicity, hopefully letting me know she was better and whatever weird thing had happened to her last night had been a result of alcohol or something she'd eaten. Maybe, in the dark, what I'd seen as scales was a bad rash and the claw hand a figment of my imagination and, well, she could have dragged her foot because she was stumbling with drunkenness.

No. Much as I tried to come up with alternatives, I didn't believe them. She'd been suffering the effects of the hex, and however cruel she'd been to hex Violet, I was going to do what I could to get rid of that thing completely. When I checked my cell phone, I saw it was Rafe calling.

I felt a spurt of pleasure as I answered. "Hi. I'm about to head down to the shop."

"Turn on your television and look at the news," he said, his tone bleak. Rafe wasn't one to utter strange and cryptic messages like that. I got a very bad feeling in my stomach.

"What's going on?" I flipped on the TV as I said it. I found a local news station and then sat down with a thump as though all the muscles in my legs had gone to sleep at once.

"Breaking news" was flashing across my screen in a red banner.

Right away I recognized Jemima's house, which was pictured on the screen. It looked even nicer in the light of day. Police cars were pulled up outside, and an earnest-looking reporter was standing outside the gate talking into the camera.

"Early this morning, police were called to the scene of a suspicious death. We have no details yet, but a young woman died here last night."

The reporter began to go on about the neighborhood and how few details there were, so I turned down the sound and said to Rafe, "That's Jemima Taft's house."

"It is."

"Did something happen to Jemima?"

"No. Her friend and William's friend, Felicity Stevens, is dead."

Horror and shock hit first. Then guilt smote me. "Dead? But I was out with them last night. She was fine." Mostly.

"Well, she's dead now."

I had to tell him. "Rafe, I think she's the one who put the hex on Violet." I gulped. I couldn't seem to get enough air. "And then we reversed it, only when you reverse a hex, sometimes it's stronger, and, ohmygod, we killed Felicity Stevens." The last bit came out somewhat hysterical.

"Why would Felicity Stevens put a hex on Violet?" And then there was the tiniest of pauses before he said, "Jealousy?"

He'd caught on a lot quicker than I had. "I think so. When they invited me to go for drinks last night, I thought they wanted to be my friends. But when I got there, Jemima was at a dinner meeting, so it was me and Felicity having a tête-à-tête, and she absolutely grilled me about William. What he liked, what he was looking for in a wife. She told me she'd fallen for him, and she seemed pretty set on separating William from his work as a butler."

"William is so much more than a butler," Rafe said, sounding annoyed.

"I know that. I'm just saying, I think she had a plan. Some-how, she found out about William's financial position. Not from me. I never said a word. She already knew he was rich. I think Jemima must have told her."

"How very indiscreet. I must say, I didn't care for Felicity Stevens, but I wouldn't have imagined her to be so ruthless."

"I guess she saw Violet as a potential rival and was so determined to clear her way to William that she put a hex on my poor cousin."

"Even with the hex being reversed, it doesn't entirely explain why she's dead."

"Sure, it does. You saw the written message. *Grow ugly, wither and die.*"

"Isn't that awfully quick work? From what I've seen of these things, they're not meant to act so quickly. People like to watch their victims suffer. As the verb wither would suggest."

He had a point. Violet had been a few days on the first stage. "Maybe when we made it more powerful, we also sped up the time frame?" I was guessing here, but it made a strange kind of sense. "I need to know more. I'm going over there."

"Don't do anything foolish, Lucy. I've got contacts within the police, as you know. Let me find out all I can. In any case, they'll never let you near the place."

"I should at least check on Jemima. She must be devastated to lose her best friend and in her house, too."

"Hold on an hour. Until we know more."

"I can't go to work." I felt like my skin wanted to jump away from my body, like it didn't want to be wrapped around someone who went around accidentally killing people.

"I'll get Clara and Mabel. They can run the shop for one day."

In fact, I knew they'd be delighted.

We ended the call, and I poured myself another cup of coffee and settled back in front of the TV, hoping for more news. Meanwhile, I was thinking furiously.

The hex. Was it really powerful enough to kill a woman?

Rafe seemed doubtful, but he hadn't been in that circle. I recalled the power I'd felt surging through my arm and the way that my athame had glowed. Maybe the blast of power that pulverized the goat skull had taken the hex to its next and final step.

Nyx jumped up on the couch and rubbed her head against my arm.

"I've never needed your help more, my little familiar. Please don't abandon me for a better witch. I didn't mean to hurt anyone. I want to be a good witch. I do."

She rubbed against me again, and I felt her warmth. Then she settled beside me, and I began to feel calmer. Soon, my breathing slowed. It was Nyx, I knew it. She'd helped me like that before.

Okay, now that I was a little calmer and oxygen was finally getting to my brain, I needed to do something. I couldn't sit on the couch watching the breaking news keep breaking over and over. There wouldn't be an update for a while, and Rafe would have it long before the media.

I looked at my phone. I could phone Margaret Twigg, but I wanted to see her face. If she watched the news, she probably already knew Felicity Stevens was dead, but she wouldn't know it was the hex that killed her. I wanted to stand in front of her when I asked exactly what she'd done. What she'd led us to do. Violet was part of this too. And Aunt Lavinia.

I called Violet next. Before I could say a word, she moaned. "Oh, Lucy. I'm really not well enough to come into work today. Being hexed, I feel like I've had a bad flu for a couple of days. I really feel quite ill and so exhausted. I wouldn't be any good to you in the shop."

Normally I'd have rolled my eyes at her attempt to get out of a day's work. But today I had other things on my mind. "Violet, Felicity Stevens is dead."

I heard her yawn, and I suspected I'd woken her up. "Felicity Stevens? Who's that?" Then, after another yawn, "Oh, that rude girl who has her claws into poor William."

At least it was some consolation to think that she barely knew the woman she'd damaged. I said, "I'm pretty sure that Felicity Stevens is the one who hexed you."

"Well, I certainly didn't warm to her. The way she was going after William was sick-making. But why would she put a hex on me?"

I went through my theory one more time.

"You think she was jealous of me and William?" She sounded more energetic all of a sudden.

"It's all I can come up with. Did you two have any kind of a run-in? Apart from you generally not liking her, is there anything I don't know?"

"No. Well, you saw her. She treated me like I was the scullery maid, which annoyed me for a start. And you should have seen her at that dinner. She was all over William. Came in the kitchen to compliment him on his food, my arse. She was fluttering her eyelashes and rubbing his arm as though she was polishing him up to put on her mantelpiece."

I thought she wasn't far wrong there.

"He seemed to like it, though. Men are such fools. When I was out front serving dinner, I'd have sworn she had her eye on the Italian, but he had absolutely no interest in her. He was more interested in Jemima Taft. So, having failed upstairs, Felicity Stevens decided to try her luck downstairs."

"With William."

She paused for a moment. "I think she succeeded, too. I got the idea that they were dating."

I hadn't told Violet that I knew they'd begun seeing each other.

Then she yawned again. "Wait, did you say she was dead?"

"Yes."

"You mean actually dead? All breath gone from her body?"

"Yes. That kind of dead." I hadn't even asked Rafe about his butler's reaction to the news. "Poor William. I never even thought to ask how he was in all of this."

"I can't imagine he was fond of that woman. She was so obvious."

I didn't share with Violet that I thought William had led a rather sheltered life for a man of his age. Instead I said, "Do you think Felicity saw you as a rival for William's affections?"

There was a long pause. Long enough that I knew she was either thinking about this very hard or trying to come up with the correct response. Finally, she said, "Possibly. We were sharing a joke when she came in to compliment him about the food. You know how he is. I think he had his arm around me, and the pair of us were laughing."

I could picture it like a scene from a movie. If this had been a movie, they'd have been just about to kiss when the rival walked in on them. Then they'd spring apart, blustering around, pretending they hadn't had that moment. Maybe the reality wasn't that far off.

"You're sure that's all you were doing? Sharing a joke? You weren't kissing or anything?"

"No. We're professionals." Then she sighed. "Besides, I don't think William sees me that way."

Actually, I thought perhaps he did. Or had. But given Violet's wretched dating history and the fact that William had never made a move, I decided to keep my mouth shut. It's amazing how often that's a good idea.

"Violet, I think that hex killed her." Then I told her about the scales and the claw and the dragging foot.

Violet, being Violet, said, "The hex? But I never meant to hurt her. I was only giving her back her own hex."

"I know. But the one who guided us and told us what to do was Margaret Twigg. I think that you and I and Aunt Lavinia should go back and confront her. We need to know exactly what we were sending back."

"I don't want to see Margaret Twigg."

"Believe me, I don't, either."

Especially as I was pretty close to accusing her of hexing a woman to death.

CHAPTER 18

"I'll fetch you and Aunt Lavinia, and we'll go together," I said to Violet.

"Do we have to?"

"Violet, a woman's dead."

"All right. I don't want to say it served her right, but people who mess with dark magic should know what they're getting into."

Apparently that rule about not speaking ill of the dead had passed my cousin by.

I picked up the two witches, and we headed to Margaret's place. Aunt Lavinia was shocked and didn't argue with me when I shared my theory that the hex had killed Felicity Stevens. Somehow, I'd hoped she'd explain why it was impossible.

We pulled up at Margaret Twigg's cottage. Even in daylight, it looked uninviting. And the mistress of the house kept up the uninviting vibe. When she opened the door, she looked as though we'd interrupted her in the middle of something that she'd much rather be doing. Like shrinking heads.

"What a surprise," she said, the *unwelcome* implied. "What do you want?"

"We need to talk to you about that hex," I said.

She let out her breath in a huff. "I can see that Violet is fully recovered. What more do you want?"

She didn't invite us in, but I walked forward until she had no choice but to forcibly stop me, which she was perfectly capable of doing, or giving in. For a moment, I thought she'd choose the former, but in the end she just took a few steps back and let us in.

"I've very little time. You'd better come into the kitchen."

Something was bubbling away on the stove smelling delicious. Great-Aunt Lavinia sniffed the air appreciatively. "Are you working on a new spell?"

"No. Rosehip jam." And she went back to stirring the fragrant, bubbling mass.

"We're here to talk about the hex that you reversed," I said.

She glanced over at me. "I reversed? I think we all did."

"Margaret, what did you do?"

She looked both puzzled and offended. "You were right there. You know perfectly well what I did. We reversed the hex that was put on Violet and very successfully too, I might add."

"Too successfully. The woman who put the hex on Violet is now dead."

I could tell she was surprised. Her eyes narrowed. "Are you certain?"

"Of course, I'm certain. It was on the news this morning."

"But the other night you didn't even know who had put the curse on Violet."

"I was with her last night. I saw it begin to work. Her skin went scaly, her fingers turned into claws, and by the end of the evening, she was dragging her foot along behind her."

Margaret appeared to consider my words. Finally, she nodded. "That could be the hex. Of course, it could be many other things too. Some kind of a neurological condition perhaps."

I stepped closer. The steam coming up from the bubbling pot put a mist in front of Margaret's face. "You know it wasn't a neurological condition. We killed that woman."

"Oh, don't be dramatic. The hex wouldn't have worked that quickly. They take their time." It was what Rafe had said, too, but I'd seen how fast Felicity went from flushed to scaly.

"Margaret, I asked you before. I'm asking you again." I pulled out my phone and pulled up the picture of the three of us at drinks only the night before. It hurt me to look at the picture of us looking so cheerful, drinking champagne as though we had everything to celebrate, when one of us would be dead the next morning. I showed her the picture. "Did you sell this woman a hex?"

She peered at the photo. "No. I've never seen either of those women before."

"Then where did she get it?"

"I'm not the only witch who sells hexes." She stopped stirring for a minute and stepped back. "I have seen something similar to that before though. It's a witch who keeps very much to herself. She sells them, lives over in Wallingford."

"Why didn't you say?"

"I didn't think it mattered."

"But the curse said wither and die. I carved those words into that black candle. Is that why Felicity is dead?"

"Oh, don't be so dramatic, Lucy. It said get ugly, first. These things take time. You saw it with Violet. It was several days, and she was only just beginning to wither."

"Are you saying given a few more days, Violet would have died? And now we reversed the curse and sent death to a woman we didn't even know?"

Margaret looked unsure of herself. It was so rare that that

worried me even more. "Frankly, I didn't expect you'd have so much power. When you pulverized that skull to dust, you may have added more potency to the hex than I had anticipated."

I sank back against her counter, almost clinging to it to keep upright. On some level, I'd worried that this would be the answer. Now the cowardly part of me wished we hadn't come here.

"I killed that girl." *First do no harm*, the words echoed around in my head. "I'll go to jail."

Margaret Twigg came over to me and put her hands on my shoulders. For the first time, she looked at me like an ally rather than an enemy. "No. You won't. We look after our own. We four were all part of this. We'll stand by you. If that woman was foolish enough to buy a curse intended to kill another woman, it's she who's responsible for the consequences, not you."

Easy words to say. Impossible for me to believe them.

I shook my head. "I have to go to the police."

"And say what? That you're a witch? That you cursed a woman to death?" She gripped my shoulders tighter now. We were no longer allies. She was back to being an adversary. "You will not. You'd set witchcraft back a hundred years. We live peaceably now. Don't start people thinking we spread evil in the world. I won't have it."

"She's right, Lucy," Aunt Lavinia said, speaking for the first time.

"No," I said, shaking my head. "She's not right. If I caused a death, I have to pay the price."

Aunt Lavinia said, "Then let the coven decide on an appropriate course of action. Not the Oxford police."

"They'll see the scales on her body and her claw hands," I reminded them.

Margaret shook her head. "Probably not. With death, the signs of the hex should have disappeared."

"For sure?"

"I said 'probably.'" Her words were tart, but I could see she was shaken.

I glanced at the phone still in my hand and our three smiling faces. "They'll soon find out I was with Felicity last night. One of the last people to see Felicity Stevens alive. I won't have to go to the Oxford police," I told them. "They'll be coming to find me."

CHAPTER 19

I promised Margaret I wouldn't do anything rash. I didn't want to, anyway. I had to think about this. And I wanted time to prepare myself in case I was arrested. I needed to organize someone to look after Nyx. Someone to look after the shop. I needed to talk to Rafe.

As I left Margaret Twigg's cottage, the need to see Rafe grew. I called him and discovered he was still at the manor house. William would be there too. I wanted to tell them what had happened with the witches.

We were a silent trio as I drove my cousin and aunt home. Aunt Lavinia got out at Vi's cottage, and neither of them invited me to come in.

Rafe had sounded grave when he said to come right over. As I rolled into the drive, the tame peacock, Henri, came forward to greet me. He seemed to have slimmed down since I had last seen him, but he most happily and greedily took the pellet from my hand that I offered him. Then he strutted off. I walked up towards the main doors of the manor house with a heavy heart.

It was Rafe who opened the door to me.

"How's William?"

"He's in shock, I think."

He took my chin in his hand. "You look so troubled, Lucy."

"It's my fault. I killed that woman. I'm sure of it." He went to speak, and I stopped him. "I got this amazing power, and it shot down my arm and through my athame and it destroyed that skull. Margaret Twigg said she hadn't expected me to have such power. I didn't mean to, but I think I made the hex too powerful. We reversed the hex and sent it back to Felicity Stevens. But it was too strong, Rafe. It killed her."

"You didn't kill Felicity Stevens, Lucy."

"You don't know that."

His expression lightened. "I do. Felicity Stevens was murdered."

Between the relief at finding I hadn't killed her and the horror that that laughing young woman who'd wanted to marry William had been murdered, I stood frozen for a minute.

Finally, taking my hand, he led me not into the drawing room where we usually sat but into the kitchen. William was sitting at the table. Olivia sat beside him, looking concerned.

"William," I said. "I'm so sorry."

Rafe was right. He did look shocked. He glanced up at me with blank eyes. "It's the oddest thing. I'm having trouble taking it in. She was so alive. And now she's gone."

I went to sit on the other side of him and put my hand on his. "Did you care for her very much?"

He shook his head. "No. That's the worst part, I think. I was going to tell her we couldn't see each other anymore. She was a nice woman. Jolly. Good company. But I couldn't picture her fitting into my future."

It was some consolation to know he hadn't fallen hard for the dead woman, but he seemed to feel guilty, as though not wanting to be with her had somehow hastened her demise.

He said, "She was going to meet me tonight. I was planning to tell her then."

"I'm so sorry."

"She seemed very taken with you," he said. "I understand you were out together last night."

"We were. And she was fun. She and Jemima. We had a wonderful time."

The stunned expression lightened for a moment as he looked puzzled. "Jemima Taft? I would never have thought of her as a fun person."

"You've only seen her in business. When she lets her hair down, she's practically a different person."

And I had the hangover to prove it.

To my surprise, Rafe made coffee. I didn't know he could make coffee. Every time I'd come here, it was always William who did the cooking and coffee-making and serving. Turned out not only could he manage to brew a decent pot of coffee, but he brought a mug over to me, already milked and sugared, exactly the way I liked it. He put coffees in front of William and Olivia too.

"Thank you," I whispered.

I drank some coffee and then felt fortified enough to ask, "How did she die?"

Rafe said, "Obviously, it's not public knowledge yet, but she was strangled."

Instinctively, I put my hand to my throat. "Strangled. But who? Why?"

"There's no clear motive yet. No culprit's been apprehended."

"What do the police know?"

"Very little. The killer used rope or line."

"What about Jemima? Is she okay?"

"As far as I know. It was her cleaners who discovered the body. She'd gone to work."

"Gone to work? Didn't she notice anything?"

He shook his head. "Jemima's bedroom is the floor above. She claims she never heard anything."

"What do you mean she claims? Do the police think she did it?" It made no sense to me. "Why would she kill her best friend?"

"No idea. Did they seem like they were having any kind of conflict last night?"

I shook my head. "Not that I could see."

"Poor girl," William said.

I stared into my coffee. "It wasn't even her house. Someone must have seen her and followed her there."

"Did anyone seem particularly interested in her last night?"

Once more I shook my head. I thought of the waiter, so attentive, gliding in and out of our sphere. Could he have developed some crazed fascination with her? The lobby bar hadn't been that busy, and no one had seemed particularly interested in us.

A bell rang in the kitchen. One of a line of servant's bells like old manor houses have. We all looked at each other, startled. Olivia said, "That's the front door. You stay here, William. I'll get it."

We stayed where we were, all of us half listening, and then Olivia reappeared with Detective Inspector Ian Chisholm and a sergeant I didn't recognize.

"Ian," I said. Probably it was a stupid thing to say, as he was here on official police business. I knew him personally, partly because he was a customer at my shop on behalf of his aunt, who was a great knitter and couldn't get out much. However, we had briefly dated. And we did seem to cross paths more often than either of us would have liked in an official capacity. As we were now.

"Lucy. I didn't expect to find you here."

"I'll go." No doubt he was here to talk to William.

He motioned me back down into my chair. "No. Stay. You were on my list anyway. This saves me a trip."

Olivia, who had smoothly stepped into William's role, said, "Coffee?"

He shook his head. "No. Thanks." Then he sat at the table. His sergeant remained standing, notepad in hand.

"I'm sure you know why I'm here."

William nodded. "The unfortunate death of Felicity Stevens, I assume."

"That's right. Can you tell us when you last saw her?"

"Yes. Yesterday morning. We met in town for a coffee."

"How did she seem?"

"The same as always. Cheerful. Full of energy and plans."

"Did she mention anything that was worrying her?"

William took a moment to think about it, then shook his head again. "No. Mind you, I didn't know her that well."

"How did you meet?"

There was a tiny pause. "She was at a dinner I catered."

He nodded as though he probably already knew this. "And who put on the dinner?"

"Jemima Taft."

He nodded. No doubt he'd already heard the story from Jemima and was checking that William's story was consistent. "And what's your relationship with Miss Taft?"

Again, that infinitesimal pause. "She's my financial advisor."

Ian spoke each word succinctly. "I understand Ms. Taft only deals with high net worth individuals. Her business card mentions bespoke wealth management."

And there it was, the reason William had been hesitating

slightly. But he had no choice. He had to tell them how he knew Felicity, and it was through Jemima. He said, "I inherited some family money."

"How fortunate," Ian said in a dry tone. "Was Felicity Stevens also a high net worth individual?"

That was an odd question. William seemed to think so too. He said, "You'd have to ask Jemima. I don't know."

"You two didn't talk about money?"

"Felicity and I? No."

"What did you talk about?"

William shrugged. "This and that. Our backgrounds. Hobbies in common. She was taking up knitting. I introduced her to Lucy."

I'm sure he hadn't meant to transfer the hot potato to me, but that effectively did it. Ian turned his gaze to me. "Yes. One minute she's buying wool, and the next minute you two are out at a swanky hotel guzzling champagne?"

He made it sound like there was something unsavory going on. I told the truth. "Felicity was starting to knit, and she brought Jemima into my shop thinking that she might take up knitting, too. We hit it off, and they invited me to meet them for drinks last night."

"At the Wainwright Hotel."

I could see what he was getting at. A knitting-shop proprietor probably wouldn't normally spend a lot of time at a hotel with those prices. "It's not my usual venue. In fact, I'd never been there before. But Jemima had a dinner meeting there, so Felicity and I had a drink in the lounge, and then Jemima joined us when her dinner was over."

"And what did you and Felicity talk about when you were alone?"

Oh man, I wished that we could do this without William sitting right there listening to every word. "We talked about being single and living in Oxford. She asked me how I came to be in Oxford. She told me about herself. Getting to know you chit-chat. She lost her job recently, and we talked about that."

I'd hoped to lead him down the path of her losing her job due to the inappropriate actions of her boss. Ian didn't follow me. "Did you talk about William?"

I wondered if Jemima had said something about Felicity's plan to bag the wealthy butler. I couldn't even look at William. "Yes. As a matter of fact, we did." I paused this time, marshaling my thoughts. "Felicity knew that William and I were friends, and she wanted to know more about him. Like I said, it was girl talk."

"And did she seem upset about anything?"

I couldn't tell him about the hex, obviously. All I said was, "She had quite a bit to drink. And at the end of the evening, she broke out in a rash. She was upset about that." He hadn't asked about whether I'd noticed scales on her body or claws for hands, so presumably Margaret was right and the hex had died with her.

"And what time did you leave the Wainwright?"

"It was about midnight. Jemima had a car hired for the evening and offered me a lift home. We dropped them off first."

"Who's we?"

"The driver and me. His name is Dick. I have his card if you need it."

He shook his head. Jemima must have given him her driver's information already.

"Did you see anyone hanging around when you dropped them off? Anything at all suspicious?"

I'd been so busy focusing on that dragging foot that I hadn't seen anything else. But I took the time now to go back in my mind and picture the area. "I think the street was deserted. I don't remember any traffic or pedestrians, but that's a very quiet, residential neighborhood. The front garden is behind a hedge, but I watched them go through and take the path to her front door. I didn't see anyone. But the driver might remember more."

He nodded. No doubt he'd managed to figure that out for himself.

"Is there anything else you noticed, Lucy? Anything at all?"

Now that I knew she'd been murdered, I no longer felt any obligation to discuss hexes and reversing of same. I shook my head. "No. I wish I could help. She was young. Had so many plans. I didn't know her very well, but I hope her killer doesn't get away with it."

He nodded and then said, "Thank you for your time."

Almost as an afterthought, he said, "After Jemima Taft joined you, you didn't notice any tension between the women? Did it seem like there was anything between them?"

He'd already asked me this. "No. I'd have said they were the best of friends. If anything, Felicity looked up to Jemima. I think Jemima was everything she wanted to be."

He turned and took a step back towards me. "What do you mean by that?"

"No doubt you've met Jemima?"

He nodded.

"I don't know if she would have been the same this morning, seeing as she'd just discovered her friend was murdered, but when I've met her, she's been cool, controlled, professional. She's wealthy and dresses impeccably. She mixes with aristocrats. Felicity is someone who wants that life. Sorry, she was someone who wanted that life. I think she was a somewhat jealous person."

In fact, if Jemima had been strangled last night, I might have suspected Felicity Stevens. I didn't say anything, but Ian obviously followed my train of thought.

"Do you think that jealousy might have been mutual? Could

you think of a reason why Jemima might have wanted to hurt her friend?"

Obviously, it was the simplest scenario. The two of them alone in that house and one killed the other. But I wasn't buying it. "No. I really don't. I think, while Felicity looked up to Jemima, Jemima saw Felicity as someone she could let her hair down with. Jemima is extremely professional and has to operate at such a high level all the time that I think Felicity was someone she trusted completely and she could be herself with." I supposed I should feel flattered that she'd trusted me enough to let loose when I'd made their duo a trio.

"All right. You've been very helpful. Thank you."

Olivia left to escort the police officers out, and we all waited, thinking our own thoughts, until she returned. Then Rafe said, "Do you think it's possible that Felicity Stevens had something on Jemima? Could she have been blackmailing her?"

"You think Felicity was blackmailing her best friend?" This was William, and he sounded horrified.

It was an awfully good theory, though. "And Jemima killed her to stop the blackmail?" I asked.

Rafe gazed across the table, as though the answers might be found by staring out the kitchen window. "It was just the two of them in that house all night, apart from the murderer."

"If there was an outside killer, how did they get in?" I asked Rafe.

I could ask him these kinds of questions because he always knew. His network of contacts was extraordinary.

"There was a main floor window open a few inches." He looked at me. "She has a cat."

I left a window open for my cat, too, but I lived on the second floor. It was impossible to install a cat door in an upper-level apartment.

But Jemima Taft should probably invest in a cat door.

CHAPTER 20

*I*t felt anticlimactic now that the police had gone. William still looked stunned, and I was torn between relief that it sounded like the hex hadn't caused Felicity's death and horror that violence had, and only hours after I had left her.

I had become so accustomed to getting involved in solving murders that it felt strange not to take a hand in this one. But it really wasn't my business.

I was about to say I should probably get back to my flat when Rafe said, "We should call a meeting of the knitting club."

"You're thinking about knitting, now?"

He flicked me a glance. "No. Theodore has some very useful contacts and a nose for digging out the truth. Even Hester, as challenging as she can be, is developing some very good skills on the computer."

"What are you getting at?"

"They could help us solve the crime."

It was true. The vampire knitting club had lots of skills between them. Not least the ability to walk around at night all but unobserved while the rest of the world slept. However, I wasn't sure getting involved was a good idea.

"Rafe. This really isn't our business."

The look he turned on me was fierce. "You were with Felicity Stevens on the last night of her life. I need to be absolutely certain that whatever provoked her killer doesn't touch you."

The normally warm kitchen suddenly felt chilly. "Why would her death affect me?"

He shook his head. "Until we know why Felicity Stevens was murdered, no one can answer that question."

"Do you think I'm in danger?"

"Probably not." Not as reassuring as absolutely not would have been. Probably left way too much wiggle room.

William looked up then and said, "Yes. I think that's a very good idea. We should try to find out what happened to poor Felicity."

That decided it. I said, "Okay. I'll head back and start setting up the back room so it's ready for our meeting tonight. You let the others know."

"No," Rafe said, stopping me in my tracks. "Let's have the meeting here. William should be part of it."

Obviously, William could have come with him to my shop. I suspected there was more going on here than he wanted to tell me. Knowing Rafe, he wanted me under his roof. And under his eye.

I often found his worry about me a little overprotective, but right now I found it endearing. I could keep busy and get through the day without dwelling too much on the murder, but once it was just me and Nyx in my flat all alone, I'd start obsessing over Felicity's death. There was a pretty good chance that Nyx would have important cat business to see to outside, which would leave me completely alone. Maybe holding the vampire knitting club at Crosyer Manor wasn't such a bad idea.

Of course, I didn't want to give in too easily. Rafe needed to know he couldn't push me around. I lifted my chin. "For

William's sake, we'll make an exception. But the vampire knitting club meets at Cardinal Woolsey's. Let's not make a habit of this."

He looked suitably reprimanded. "Agreed."

William made my concession completely worthwhile by looking up and saying, "Thanks, Lucy. I know she wasn't my girlfriend or anything, but she was a friend. I don't think I can rest until we've at least tried to find out what happened to her. And even better, stopped the killer in their tracks."

Rafe seemed very relieved. "Why don't you stay for the afternoon. Work on your knitting. Let William cook for you. I also want to show you some of the passages I've translated in that extraordinary book I showed you."

I rose. "I can't. I need to make sure things are okay at the shop. And I have a couple of things to do."

William said, "Will you come back for dinner? It will do me good to have somebody to cook for. I'll make dinner for you and Olivia."

I could hardly turn down an offer like that. Especially as I understood that cooking soothed William. I thought it was how he made sense of the world. So I agreed.

"I'd better get going, then, so I can be back in time for dinner."

Something about my tone made Rafe look at me sharply. "What are you intending?"

Darn it, he could read me like a book. "Nothing." Which of course immediately made me sound like I was planning something.

His gaze settled on my face, and then he said, "No."

I grew immediately huffy. "What do you mean no?"

"No. You're not to go and see Jemima Taft. I forbid it."

Naturally, I grabbed onto the last bit of that sentence. "You forbid it? Who are you, my dad?" Not that my father could stop me doing anything anyway. I was an adult. Nearly thirty, for goodness' sake.

"Lucy, Jemima Taft is the most likely person to have murdered Felicity Stevens. You're not to go near her. Let the police do their job."

"Says he who just called a meeting of the vampire knitting club to figure out who killed William's friend." Ha, I had him there.

"That's different. We're a group of friends trying to solve a murder with the clues and knowledge at hand. We aren't pushing ourselves into the path of the murderer."

I shook my head. "Jemima Taft is no more a murderer than I am. Besides, she probably needs a friend."

The thought that that very cool, poised woman might turn to me was a bit ridiculous. No doubt she had hundreds of posh friends to lean on. Still, she and I were the only two people who had been with Felicity last night. I felt like we should hash out the evening and see if there'd been something that happened or some clue Felicity had dropped that I'd missed and maybe Jemima had caught.

While these thoughts were going through my head and I was trying to figure out how to express them, my mobile phone rang. I didn't know the number, but I answered it anyway. It was a local Oxford number.

"Hello, Lucy speaking."

"Lucy. This is Jemima Taft." Her voice sounded higher-pitched and jittery. Which I perfectly understood.

"Jemima! I was just thinking about you. I heard what happened. I'm so sorry."

Of course, I had the rapt attention of everyone at the table now. I could feel them all staring at me—Olivia with general curiosity, William with what looked like hope that Jemima could help us solve this thing, and Rafe with consternation.

He was already shaking his head at me when she said, "Look, it's ghastly here. The police are crawling all over my house. I don't know what to do with myself. Could we go somewhere and talk?"

I could imagine how awful it was for her. "I completely understand. I want to talk to you too and go over everything that happened last night."

"Exactly. All my other friends will be plucking at me and wanting to know all the details that I don't want to talk about. You were there. I don't have to fill you in on anything."

Okay, not exactly the comforting sharing of information that I had hoped for, but oddly, I did understand what she meant. Plus, from her perspective, the fact that I wasn't a close friend of Felicity meant I wouldn't be able to reminisce about our shared childhoods and school days and make her sad. My reminiscences were scanty, to say the least.

Even if Rafe hadn't been horrified at the thought of me and Jemima getting together, I wasn't completely stupid. I wouldn't invite her to my flat, say, where we'd be all alone. She must be one of the top suspects because of the circumstances of her friend's death. I didn't think she'd killed her friend, but I wouldn't be hanging out with her in dark alleys, either.

She said, "I'll meet you anywhere. Just, please, nowhere the press are likely to find us."

I thought for a second and then said, "I know the perfect spot. Elderflower Tea Shop. It's right beside Cardinal Woolsey's on Harrington Street. It's tucked away. No one would think to look for you there."

"What about the owner? Might they call the press just to get their establishment's name in the newspaper?"

Wow, that was cynical. She definitely moved in a different circle than I did. Or the Miss Watts. I reassured her that Florence and Mary Watt were in their eighties and much more interested in whether today's scones were as light and fluffy as yesterday's scones than they were in the local news.

"Very well. I'll meet you there in an hour."

"Perfect. See you then."

I hung up, and Rafe immediately exploded. "Are you insane? You can't meet that woman."

"We won't be alone. You heard me. We're meeting at Elder-flower. There will be loads of people there."

He was looking at me through narrowed eyes. "It's my belief you used your magic to cause her to phone you."

"Nope. She really did want to talk to me."

"Just so long as she's not some peculiar serial killer who likes to do away with young blondes who are her competition."

I shook my head. "That theory doesn't really hold water. She and Felicity were friends. If she were so jealous, she wouldn't have gone drinking with her so often and had her to stay at her house."

"Still, I don't like it."

I narrowed my gaze at him and leaned over so that for once I was towering above him, since he was still sitting down and I was standing up. "Do not even think about following me to the tea shop." I could see he planned on it. I raised my finger and wagged it at him. "I'm serious. I do not want to see you there."

William said, "You can't go anyway, Rafe. Jemima Taft will recognize you. Remember, we met here when she was planning her dinner."

He looked quite put out. "Very well. Then Olivia must go." Olivia jumped in her seat, obviously not having expected to hear her name.

"Me?"

"Jemima Taft doesn't know you, does she?"

"No," William said. "That's a good idea. Olivia and I have always dealt with different financial advisors. It seemed more prudent. And you weren't in the house when Jemima came to arrange the dinner."

"I don't need a babysitter," I exclaimed.

"Please, don't make me more worried than I already am," Rafe said.

"Fine. But be discreet. She's already paranoid that reporters are following her. If you seem too interested in us, she'll bolt."

"I understand. I'll sit far away from you and..." She turned to Rafe. "I'm not sure what I am supposed to do?"

"Keep an eye on them. If Lucy appears to be in any danger, call me immediately."

"Or the police," I added.

"I'll get there sooner," he countered.

That ended the argument because I knew he was right.

CHAPTER 21

$\mathcal{I}$ headed back to my shop. That is to say, I drove up, parked my little red car around the back of the building, and then I walked back around to the front so I could peek in the shop window. As I had imagined, Clara and Mabel had things well under control.

There were three customers in Cardinal Woolsey's. Mabel had one, Clara had another, and the third seemed perfectly happy browsing crochet cottons.

The two vampires would be full of news when we met up tonight for the knitting club. The only downside was my grandmother would feel left out. I knew it was hard for her that she, who had built Cardinal Woolsey's from nothing and loved it as much as I did, could never help out while her other undead friends could.

One of these days, Gran would find a new place to live and perhaps open another knitting shop. Somewhere she wasn't known. Mostly she stayed in Oxford for me, and for now that suited both of us.

Knowing things in Cardinal Woolsey's were well under control, I walked back around the building and entered my flat from the main door. Up one set of stairs and I was in the main living area and kitchen floor. Nyx seemed gratifyingly glad to see me. I was half tempted to open the door between my flat and the shop so she could enjoy her customary spot in the front window, but if I did that, then Mabel and Clara would know I was up here, and I needed a little time to myself to make sense of things.

Felicity Stevens was dead, and I was one of the last people who'd seen her alive. It was shocking. A little bit frightening. At least the hex hadn't killed her. But then what, or who, had?

I fed Nyx, and we spent some time commiserating with each other about yet another murder. For two such peaceable creatures, Nyx and I seemed to be embroiled in a lot of unpleasantness. I suspected she blamed me. I suspected she was right.

While I was alone, I also took some quiet time to center myself and recite a spell of protection. That helped. I knew I was meeting the woman who could turn out to be Felicity's killer. My instinct told me it wasn't her, but my instincts weren't infallible.

However, I wasn't a complete fool. Jemima didn't know I was a witch. I had powers. And I was on my guard. Besides, why would she want to hurt me? But then why would anyone have wanted to harm Felicity? The whole thing didn't make any sense.

I'd discovered in the past, though, that what was incomprehensible to begin with became clear by asking the right questions and separating truth from lie, fact from fiction, misdirection from truth. I'd start with Jemima Taft.

Why was she really meeting me? Perhaps she had misdirection in mind. I'd need to listen carefully, not only to what she did say but what she didn't.

I headed back out in time to meet Jemima at the tea shop and found her standing outside the door to Elderflower. She was wearing a long, black wool coat and a black woolen hat. It wasn't very busy on a late January afternoon, but a few shoppers were about, and students often walked down this street. I found her scrutinizing Elderflower's menu, though it was obviously an excuse to keep her face averted from passersby.

"Jemima," I said softly.

She turned. "Lucy, I'm so glad you came. Thank you." She looked a little pale but otherwise her usual impeccable self.

"Of course. I really wanted to talk to you as well." I made a motion to go into the tea shop, and she grabbed my wrist.

"Could we go for a walk or something? I look so dreadful today. I don't feel up to being seen in any sort of public venue, even as insignificant as a tea shop."

The Miss Watts might not feel that their tea shop was quite as inconsequential as she seemed to think. Besides, Olivia was supposed to keep an eye on me. She couldn't very well do that if I didn't turn up.

I looked at Jemima, but she looked better than me on my best day.

"You look beautiful," I said.

"Please." She glanced up and down the street as though afraid she might be overheard. "I've had nothing but police and comings and goings and noise all day."

Not to mention her best friend murdered in her house, which weirdly seemed to bother her less than that her day had been interrupted by the cops.

"Sure. Let's go for a walk."

I needed to let Olivia know that I wouldn't be turning up or there'd be a vampire search party prowling all over Oxford for me. I told Jemima that the ladies who owned Elderflower were friends of mine, which was true, and that I'd asked them to save us a table, which wasn't. "I don't like to let them hold one of their best tables if we're not going to use it. I'll just run up and tell them we won't be needing it."

Not waiting for her to give me an answer, I went into the tea shop, and fortunately Mary Watt was seating people today. She looked delighted to see me, as she always did.

"Lucy. What a delightful surprise."

I felt awful. I'd have loved to stay. The smell of baking made me hungry. "I'm so sorry. I had planned to bring a friend here. But she's not feeling well, so we're going to go for a walk."

She looked a bit puzzled. "All right, dear. Of course."

"The thing is, a woman named Olivia will be arriving very soon. Could you let her know that my friend wasn't feeling well and we've gone for a walk?"

"Of course."

I turned away and all but bumped into Olivia, who'd come in behind me. Quickly I explained the situation to her. And we stood there, both uncertain what to do next. She said, "That's awkward. Couldn't you talk Jemima Taft into staying?"

I shook my head. "She's feeling really shaken up from the morning. Says she wants to stretch her legs and get some air. Look, nothing is going to happen to me in broad daylight walking with a friend. Rafe's completely overprotective."

"He may be, but he's also my employer, and he gave me very strict instructions not to let you out of my sight."

I let out an infuriated breath. Not my first where Rafe was concerned, and almost undoubtedly, it wouldn't be my last. "I take full responsibility for my own safety. Perhaps you could remind your employer that I am an independent adult."

She looked amused. "I don't think it'll do any good. Not where you're concerned."

I was so shocked, my mouth fell open. "What? Because he thinks I'm a child? Incompetent?"

"No, silly. Because he's in love with you."

Well, that shut me up, didn't it?

But not for long. "I don't care what you tell him. Just don't follow me."

"I don't think I'd be very good at surveillance. I'm a gardener. This cloak and dagger stuff makes me nervous. Besides, the weeping willows at Crosyer Manor need their lower branches trimming. I always do it at this time of year." That seemed to decide her on abandoning her post as my bodyguard.

I went back outside and found Jemima had slipped a pair of sunglasses on. It wasn't sunny. Was she trying to disguise her appearance?

We headed off towards University Parks, a large green space with playing fields, gardens and running and walking paths that wound through the gardens and followed the path of the Cherwell River. Between watching out for bicycles, other pedestrians and traffic, we kept our conversation to the merest pleasantries until we were through the gate and on one of the paths.

Jemima burst out, "It's been absolutely ghastly today."

My heart stirred in sympathy. "It must have been awful. Was it you who found her?" I knew it wasn't, but I didn't want her to suspect I had a secret source of information. She was freaking out as it was.

She shook her head. "Actually, it was my cleaning staff. They come in once a week. I often leave Felicity sleeping when she's stayed the night. I like to be at work early, and she preferred to sleep in."

"Did she have a key?"

"Oh yes."

"What time did you leave this morning?"

"About half past six."

She'd left the house at six-thirty? She hadn't even arrived home until after midnight last night. The woman must need very little sleep. "And you didn't see Felicity before you left or hear her?"

She shook her head. "No. I assumed she was sleeping." Her face twisted in. "But now, I imagine she was already dead."

"And you never heard anything in the night?"

A couple walking their dog came towards us, and she waited until after they'd passed and we were out of earshot. "I did hear something. I think she was on the phone. That was shortly after we got home. I hadn't gone up to bed yet. I was getting some water, and she was already in her room."

"But that could have been her murderer. Did you hear what she said? Any idea who it was?"

She turned to look at me. "I think it was William."

I wanted to yell no. William hadn't killed Felicity. He wouldn't kill anyone. It was rather unfortunate that she'd called him, though. "And you told the police this?"

She hesitated. "No. I didn't."

"But you have to. We both know William wouldn't hurt a fly. But if you heard him on the phone with Felicity and don't say anything, it seems as though you think he could have hurt her."

While I was speaking, her eyes went hard. "William Thresher is a client, and my clients are everything to me. They come to me for my loyalty and discretion. I would never betray one of them. Anyway, I couldn't be absolutely positive it was William I heard her speaking to. You saw the condition she was in last night. She was slurring her words and talking rubbish."

There was that.

"And in any case, the police will no doubt access her mobile phone records and find out for themselves who she called."

She was right. The police would soon discover who Felicity had phoned late last night. Besides, William hadn't said anything about a call, so it couldn't have been him on the phone.

Instead of wasting time on a fruitless argument, I decided to ask what had happened after I'd last seen the two of them. She seemed quite happy to talk about that. "After your driver dropped you and Felicity off, you went into the house. Did you see anyone? Hear anything?"

There was a spurt of laughter that she quickly cut off, probably because it was inappropriate. "You saw the state Felicity was in. Swaying and so drunk she couldn't even walk properly. I certainly didn't have any attention to spare for looking around the garden. No. I didn't see anyone."

Then she looked over at me. "Did you?"

I shook my head. "It was the same for me. I was watching to make sure you both got into the house all right. And then your driver kindly dropped me off home."

"Dick's paid to do what I tell him to," she reminded me.

We walked on, and she let out a sound of frustration. "This couldn't happen at a worse time. I'm working flat out. I've got a very delicate deal closing."

Was she seriously thinking that her friend's murder was an inconvenience to her business?

I tried to go easy on her, knowing that shock and stress didn't necessarily bring out the best in people. No doubt thoughts she'd have normally kept in her head were popping out of her mouth unbidden.

"You were her best friend. Can you think of anyone who would want to hurt Felicity?"

"Obviously not. The police have asked me the same thing."

"What about her former employer? The art gallery owner who was inappropriate? She told me the whole story last night when you were at dinner."

For three or four steps, she didn't say a word. We were getting close to the river now, and I glimpsed a swan gliding past, white and serene.

"I'm not entirely sure we got the full story there," she said at last. "Obviously, she was my friend, and I'm gutted that she's dead, but Felicity wasn't always truthful about things."

"Oh." Somehow this didn't surprise me.

"I think it's possible she was the one who was inappropriate. Peter Bedworth is very rich, you see."

"Her former employer?"

"Yes. Felicity has—had—an obsession about marrying a wealthy man. It was very sad. She had all the benefits of a top education and mixing with a certain class of people, but really the family didn't have the money to support the lifestyle she learned to believe should be hers. She wanted it very badly."

We'd reached the river now and turned to follow along its banks. "I noticed whenever I saw you two together that she was, well, frankly, I thought she was trying to be you. And not quite succeeding."

"They do say imitation is the sincerest form of flattery. I suppose she's flattered me as long as I've known her. We'd been friends since boarding school, you see."

"Could Peter Bedworth have hurt Felicity?"

She seemed to consider my words. "I suppose it's possible. I wouldn't have said he'd want to get rid of her permanently though. He let her go from her job, paid her a decent severance. Why would he?"

"What if she wasn't finished with him?" I was thinking hard. "Could it have been Peter Bedworth you heard on the phone last night? Maybe she called him to tell him she wanted a bigger severance package?"

"You've got a suspicious mind."

"Someone killed Felicity," I reminded her.

She put her hands out. "Don't you think I've been trying to work out who could have murdered my friend? I'm wondering about my house cleaners. What if they were nicking things in my home and Felicity surprised them? Might they kill her?"

That seemed like a stretch. "You didn't trust your cleaners?" And yet she left them alone in her home every week.

"I'd have said they were completely honest. They've worked

for me for three years. But does one ever know the people one employs?" Did she know how utterly snobby and entitled she sounded? No doubt Oxford CID would check out the cleaners, in any case.

As we were walking, I got a funny feeling in the back of my neck—a tingling. If I hadn't been thinking about murder and danger, I might have disregarded the sensation, but my senses were definitely on high alert. I scanned the immediate vicinity and saw nothing more alarming than a goose that was glaring at us as though we were invading his space.

I turned and glanced behind me and saw a chubby gentleman in a tweed blazer and a wide-brimmed hat. A pair of binoculars hung from his neck, and he carried a bag of wild birdseed. Just an Oxford stroller with nothing but birdwatching on his mind.

Theodore.

CHAPTER 22

heodore looked back at me blandly as though he had no idea who I was and was only on this path to do a spot of birdwatching.

I couldn't tell him off or send back a very rude message to Rafe. I had to turn around and pretend we weren't being followed.

"Is there anyone else who would have wanted to hurt Felicity that you can—"

She put up a hand to stop me. Her mobile was going off. She answered it, cool and crisp, for all the world as though she were sitting at her desk.

I only heard her half of the conversation, obviously, but she said, "I can't talk now. Bring the documents to the office. I'll meet you there in an hour."

She clicked off and said, "Sorry about that." And then in a rush, "I really can't be away from work this long. I'm going to have to go back."

I felt my eyes widen. "On the day your friend was murdered? Are you sure you're up for it?"

"Well, it's a dreadful thing, obviously. But I can't bring her back. And this is a very big deal. It must be done quickly." She glanced behind us, but Theodore had the binoculars to his eyes and seemed engrossed in avian fascination. "If anyone got wind of this deal, the whole thing could blow up. These things require absolute finesse and complete discretion."

I turned to stare at her. Did she not remember that she'd already told us all about the deal? I decided to test a theory. "Is that the Hurst and Havers deal?" I asked airily, as though it was something I'd read in the Oxford paper.

She stopped walking. She actually stopped dead, and I took two steps before I'd realized. Her eyes were wide, and she looked deathly pale. "How did you hear that?"

"You told me. Don't you remember?"

She gripped my wrist so hard it hurt. "I would never tell you any such thing. It would be completely inappropriate. I could lose my job."

"Honestly. That is how I found out. You'd had a few drinks, and you told us last night. Don't you remember?"

She closed her eyes for a minute and then opened them. "No. I don't."

I didn't want to suggest she possibly had a problem with alcohol, not when she could party till after midnight and be at work at six-thirty the next morning, but if she was having memory lapses, that couldn't be good.

"I must ask you to promise me not to breathe a word of this. Not to a soul."

"I wouldn't. That's not my world. I deal in cashmeres and silks and cottons. Your world is a million miles away."

"Nevertheless, it was most indiscreet." She put a hand to her head. "It's the stress, you see."

It had looked to me like it was the booze. Though I could understand that a really high-pressure job might encourage her to drink too much.

A cold chill went over my skin as I wondered whether Rafe was right. Maybe Felicity had tried to blackmail her best friend over the Hurst and Havers deal. Maybe she'd appreciated how sensitive the information was that Jemima was blabbing in the bar. Had she tried to get money out of her friend in order to keep her mouth shut? And had that friend decided to silence her permanently?

Now I wished I'd kept my mouth shut. She knew that I knew all about her secret deal, just like Felicity had known. I was suddenly glad that Theodore was only a few paces behind us. He'd be on me in a second if I made so much as a squeak.

But Jemima didn't seem like she was going to get violent with me. She looked like she wanted to smack herself.

She quickened her pace. "Look, sorry, but I've got to get back to work. I've called Dick to pick me up at the entrance to the park. Can you make your own way back?"

"Okay. Sure." So much for our bonding and mutual grieving time. I'd been dumped for a business deal.

She sped up the pace so we got a nice, healthy workout as we speed-walked our way back towards Parks Street.

As though it had appeared by magic, the familiar black Mercedes eased around, and before she got in, she grabbed my wrist in a vice-like grip one more time. "You promised me, Lucy. Remember that. You do not breathe a word of that deal to anyone."

"I won't tell a living soul," I promised her. Neatly leaving out the possibility of sharing with the undead. "Anything you or Felicity said to me is in the vault." Then I had to modify that statement. "Except anything about Felicity that might help the police. But I've already been interviewed by them. I doubt they'll be asking me any more questions."

She'd obviously lost interest after she got my promise. She

already had the door open, having waved Dick back when he tried to get out of his door.

I stood there and watched as the car fit smoothly back into traffic, and then she was gone. I didn't have long to wait before Theodore arrived at my side.

"You're birdwatching now?"

"Very relaxing hobby," he said placidly, as though it really could be a coincidence he was here. "I was watching a flock of waxwings eating the rowan berries. Lovely birds. From Scandinavia, you know."

It was impossible to stay mad at Theodore. Anyway, it wasn't his fault he'd been tasked with following me. Besides, if Jemima had turned out to be a psycho killer, I'd have been happy to have his help. As it was, she had a deal to put to bed. After that was done, might a psycho killer emerge? Did I have to watch my back?

I told Theodore what she had said and, holding to my promise, said there were details of the deal I couldn't share. "Do you think Felicity tried to squeeze money out of her and provoked Jemima into a murderous rage?"

"Possible, I suppose," Theodore said. "What else did you discover? Anything more about our victim?"

I told him about the gallery and the two different stories that had emerged about Felicity's former employer. One that she herself had told and the different variation that Jemima suspected was closer to the truth.

"Peter Bedworth, you say," Theodore said. "I know the gallery. Very exclusive. Need an appointment to get in."

"And are you thinking of making such an appointment?"

"Exactly. I'll see you back at Crosyer Manor, Lucy."

"Are you going there now?"

He looked at me as though I'd been in a hot sun too long. "In these clothes? I must go home, get properly attired and see if Sylvia will lend me the Bentley."

Nyx and I arrived back at Crosyer Manor in plenty of time for dinner. In spite of a pretty harrowing day, and one that had started out with a hangover to boot, one of William's fabulous meals would go a long way to helping improve my mood.

I suspected preparing the meal would be good therapy for William, too. And, since I had missed the tea and scone that I'd been looking forward to at Elderflower Tea shop, I was definitely ready to eat.

When I got out of my car, Henri waddled forward in search of treats. I let Nyx out, and the two stared at each other. An interesting standoff. One pure black and sleek and wiry, coiled with energy, the other pudgy and as colorful as a jeweler's window. Then Nyx hissed, and Henri, not to be outdone, let out the raucous squawk so at odds with the beautiful plumage of a peacock. He didn't even stay for his treat. He turned and waddled off.

Satisfied that she had rid her space of yet more vermin, Nyx padded daintily to the front door of the manor house. It was opened by Olivia.

"Dinner's going to be late, I'm afraid," she said, looking worried.

"Why? What's going on?" I tried to quell the hollowness in the pit of my stomach and to concentrate on her words.

"It's William. He hadn't noticed, but there was a message on his mobile phone from Felicity. She must have left it last night. It was rather drunk and rambling, but she all but proposed to him. He's very upset."

I swallowed hard. Poor William. What an awful thing to get a message from someone right before she was murdered. "What did it say? Were there any clues?"

"I don't know. He called the police right away, of course. They've been with him all afternoon. But he feels terrible. He believes that if he'd picked up the phone, she'd still be alive. Maybe she was trying to tell him something or there was someone with her who perhaps wouldn't have committed that terrible crime if they'd known William was listening in."

"Wow. That's a lot of ifs. And a lot of responsibility that William's putting on himself."

She nearly sagged with relief. "Thank goodness. You sound like Rafe. I think he needs to hear that same message from another person. He's my older brother, so he won't listen to me. And William was born responsible. He was trained to take on the huge task of running Crosyer Manor and keeping Rafe safe. He's got an overdeveloped sense of duty, and with it, I'm afraid, comes self-blame."

Honestly, if Felicity Stevens hadn't been dead, I'd have been tempted to give her a piece of my mind. What had she been doing messing up a nice guy like William? He deserved a nice woman who cared about him and would take an interest in Rafe and Olivia and this estate. It was a tall order for any woman, but as Felicity had made plain to me, she'd never intended to be a real partner. I was pretty sure she'd seen William as a never-empty cash machine.

I handed Olivia my coat and headed inside. "You'll find him in the kitchen," she said. As though she had to tell me that. I might not have lived with William his whole life, but I knew where he felt safe.

It had been jarring to see Rafe in the kitchen with his staff this morning, but now it seemed normal to find him here. He glanced up at me and looked relieved. "Lucy. You're home." He came forward and kissed me, then whispered, "Do what you can with him. I've failed miserably."

William's stunned expression hadn't dissipated. If anything, he looked worse. His eyes looked hollow, and his complexion was gray.

The phone sat in front of him, and he stared it as though Felicity might call again.

I appreciated Rafe's confidence in me, but really, what could I do?

I went and sat beside William and put my hand over his. "I heard. I'm so sorry."

Naturally, I was dying to hear what was on that recording, but I wanted to be delicate.

Luckily, Rafe wasn't at all worried about being delicate. He said, "Play that message for Lucy."

CHAPTER 23

*R*afe could have ordered William to do anything. Take off all his clothes and run around the house naked, cook mashed potatoes out of a box, and William would have done it. He was that stunned. He obediently pushed play, and I had the unpleasant experience of hearing a dead woman's voice. Make that a drunk, dead woman's voice.

"William," she said. Even "William" was slurred. It reminded me of Violet trying to talk when she'd lost the tooth, and for a second I wondered if that indignity had been added to the other ones piled on poor Felicity as the hex began to take hold. She continued, her speech slurred but comprehensible. "Need to see you. I'm in love with you. Tomorrow seems so far away. I think about you all the time. Something important to tell you." Then some muttering or coughing before her voice grew clear once more. "I know you're a bit shy and probably want to take things slow, but I don't. Want to marry you." And then there was the sound of something dropping and her swearing, and then, "Call me."

And that was it. The words had been slurred and stumbling but clear enough for all that.

"She said she had something to tell me," he said, looking at me as though I might know what it was. "What if it was the thing that got her killed? If only I'd answered my phone."

"William. It must have been nearly one in the morning by the time she called you."

"It was one-twelve, to be precise," Rafe put in.

I nodded thanks. "After one in the morning. No one could be expected to answer their mobile at that time. And anybody who wasn't, well, pretty drunk would have realized that. Everybody puts their phone on do not disturb at night. And you have to get up early. You have a job."

"I'm not turning my phone off at night anymore. From now on, if anybody needs to get hold of me in the middle of the night, I shall be there. What kind of a friend did I turn out to be?"

I said, "Did it occur to you that the thing she wanted to say was the thing she then said? I think I'm in love with you and I want to marry you? Which, by the way, I do not believe."

He looked like I'd smacked him a couple of times. "I didn't give her a proper chance. I was going to end things, and she wanted to marry me. I feel dreadful. I could have been kinder."

"You were more than kind. I'm not saying this to upset you, but hopefully it will make you feel a bit better. She really wanted to marry a wealthy man. I'm not saying she wouldn't rather have you than some old, wrinkled guy with no teeth, but she wasn't falling in love with your pretty blue eyes."

He looked relieved for a second and then shook his head. "You're only saying that to make me feel better."

William already had so much modesty, such a relatively low opinion of himself, that I didn't know how to say, "No, dude, she seriously only wanted your money" without crushing him. I was doing the best I could here.

This time, it was Olivia who helped me out. "Are you saying that woman was nothing but a gold digger?"

Oh, yes. Nailed it. I nodded, talking to Olivia now, but of course my words were intended for William. "She talked about money and wealth a lot. She definitely wanted to marry up, as they say."

"But I'm not 'up,'" William argued. "I'm a butler."

"Estate manager," Rafe corrected.

Again, I felt bad repeating what Felicity had said, but if sharing girl talk would help dispel the gray sadness in William's eyes, I'd spill. "Felicity told me she wanted you to give up working for Rafe."

"What?" two male voices said in unison.

"I know. She scoffed, called you a servant and said Rafe had better start looking for a new butler."

Now William started to get some color back in his cheeks. The ruddy look of anger. "I'd never leave my position. I'm certain I made that clear to Felicity."

"That's why she was so eager to have drinks with me last night. She was trying to find out whether you'd ever leave Rafe." I glanced from man to master. "I told her you wouldn't."

"Quite right. Naturally, I could never tell a woman about the peculiar nature of my work." He leaned back and looked wretched. "Which makes it incredibly difficult to get serious about dating."

Olivia looked angry, obviously on her brother's behalf. "I know you're not supposed to speak ill of the dead, but I didn't like Felicity Stevens. And I didn't think she was right for you, William," she said, gripping her brother's shoulder.

"I agree," Rafe said.

"Make that three of us," I added.

William shifted his gaze from the ceiling to look at all of us in turn. "I'm well aware she wasn't right for me. Any fool could see that. But I should have been kinder."

He was too nice for his own good.

"What did the police say?" I asked him.

"Just a lot of searching questions about our relationship. Since she was talking about marriage on that message, they seemed to think I was lying when I said it was casual. We kept going over the same ground again and again."

Suddenly he seemed to gather himself together and glanced up at the big clock. "Oh. The chicken will be dry. I'm sorry. I'd nearly forgotten."

"No. It doesn't matter." He'd had an emotional day. "We could get takeout."

Everyone laughed, even William. "They don't exactly deliver pizza way out here," Rafe informed me.

"Right."

William said, "Look, you two go and sit in the lounge and have a drink. I'll call you when dinner's ready."

I didn't care if Rafe was his employer and he was the servant. I said, "I'm only eating in the dining room if you're joining us." I didn't think he should be sitting here alone brooding. At least if he joined us at the dinner table, I could make sure he actually ate something.

I could see he was about to refuse when Rafe said, "I agree. In fact, I insist you both join us for dinner. You know what they say about murders. If they're not solved within twenty-four hours, the chances of apprehending the culprit go down exponentially. You knew Felicity Stevens better than anyone except, perhaps, Lucy, so you may have noticed things that didn't seem important but could help solve her murder."

It was after six now. We knew that Felicity had been killed sometime between one-twelve in the morning when she'd called William and whenever the cleaners found her. Drat, I should have asked Jemima what time that was. I'd been assuming she was killed in the middle of the night. But perhaps she'd been killed in the morning. Maybe Jemima was right and the cleaners had done it.

I went to sit in the living room. Nyx was way ahead of me, already curled up on one of the priceless couches that she had now turned into a very elegant cat bed. Rafe offered me wine or anything I wanted out of his bountiful liquor cabinet, but I shook my head. I wanted to keep a clear head tonight.

The vampire knitting club were an odd collection, but they had a knack of talking through problems, and sometimes they'd say exactly the right thing at the right moment to cut through the clouds and reach the sunshine of truth. I wanted to be alert enough to catch those moments.

I chose sparkling water, and Rafe prepared it himself, even popping in a fresh lemon slice. While the English preferred their drinks lukewarm, there was always a bucket of ice for me. He popped three cubes into the glass and passed me my fizzy drink. Then he sat down on the settee beside me. Nyx immediately roused herself out of the deepest slumber and came over to settle in his lap.

"I'm sorry she's so clingy," I said.

He glanced up at me and back down at the cat. "It makes a nice change."

Ouch.

There was an awkward silence. I sipped my drink and heard the ice cubes rattle around.

"Time of death was approximately three a.m., by the way," he said. He must have known I was staring, for his lips quirked up in a half-smile. "I had a feeling you were wondering."

I asked what condition the body was in.

"Cause of death was strangulation. With a plastic cord. It was clean and quick. Almost like she was garroted."

I swallowed. Just hearing that word made my throat hurt. "Any clue where the rope came from?"

"Oh yes. From Jemima's laundry room. It was a clothesline."

"Jemima as the murderer fits with the theory that her friend thought she'd make a quick buck by blackmail."

"It does. Very stupid murderer though, to do the deed in her own house, using her own laundry line."

"When they found the body, was it..." I trailed off.

"All traces of the hex were gone, if that's what you mean."

It was. "So Margaret was right. The hex ended with death."

"This one, anyway."

"As awful as it is, I'm glad that Violet and Margaret and I, and poor Aunt Lavinia, didn't turn out to be responsible."

He looked at me very seriously. "Far be it from me to lecture you, but there's a lesson to be learned here."

I nodded. I was way ahead of him. "I can't take part in spells with Margaret, not when I don't even know what they are. The four of us together are very powerful."

"You on your own are very powerful. I suspect, and I believe you do too, that in reversing a curse, you could have turned something that was painful and unpleasant into something lethal."

"I didn't mean to."

"Of course not. Nevertheless..."

Point taken.

William sent Olivia in to call us to the table, and not many minutes later, he walked in bearing three plates: one for Olivia, one for me and one for him. For Rafe, he poured a glass of wine, a deep, rich burgundy.

I would have said William Thresher was not capable of making a bad meal. I'd have been wrong. The chicken was over-cooked and tough, he'd burned the potatoes, and the vegetables were cooked to mush.

I didn't say anything. I was too grateful to get a meal.

One bite in and William reached for our plates. "This is inedible. Lucy, Olivia, I can only apologize."

I grabbed his wrist before he could get his fingers on my plate. "Take my food away and die," I said. "I'm too hungry to care."

Olivia nodded. "It's fine, William. We know you're under stress."

He looked very distressed. "A man has his standards," he said.

"You can make it up to us. I'll expect a fabulous, perfectly cooked meal next time you invite me for dinner."

"I'm only grateful you'll give me another chance." He sawed into his own chicken with exaggerated vigor as though he were in my country cutting down a redwood.

However, as merely adequate as the food was, I think we all felt better for eating. We adjourned to the lounge for coffee and didn't have too long to wait before the vampires began to show up for knitting club.

Normally we started at ten o'clock, but given the circumstances, everybody was there and ready to go by nine. I had to give them credit, though. Rafe had called this meeting with sleuthing in mind, but every single one of them brought their knitting. Which meant that I had to haul my sorry mess of a rug out of the bag and sit there and pretend like I was going to knit.

Clara sat beside me and swapped projects as she had done the first night. I didn't think anybody was going to be fooled, but at this point, I didn't really care. The only chance that rug had of ever feeling my feet on it was if someone else knit it.

Rafe, presumably since we were gathered at his home, took charge of the meeting right away. "I assume, given the nature of this evening's meeting, that we can dispense with our usual project update."

Hester made a sound of mingled fury and frustration. "But I just finished a coat. And it wasn't easy, let me tell you. I want to show—"

"We'll meet again Thursday, Hester. You can show us then."

Silence Buggins, never one to let a pause be birthed, jumped in and said, "Do you have any idea what tiny stitches I've had to use to knit myself a proper undervest? I used a variety of techniques which you will never see once I begin wearing the undergarment."

She was about to embark on showing her project anyway when Rafe gently stopped her. "Thursday, Silence. We'll look forward to hearing about it on Thursday."

She sniffed, and a very rare thing happened. She and Hester shared a glance that showed them united on the same side for once. Hester even moved to sit beside Silence and said, "You can show me it when we have a break."

"And I'd be very pleased to admire your work," Silence replied.

Rafe quickly laid out everything we knew about the murder. Theodore described his meeting with Peter Bedworth, the art gallery owner, and said, "As much as the man seemed pleased to be rid of Felicity Stevens, he didn't seem to have any grudge to hold. In fact, he hadn't heard about her death. When I told him, he seemed rather sad." Theodore checked his notebook. "He'd known her family, you see. It's how she got the job in the first place. Seemed very sorry to hear the news."

We all thought about that for a minute. "That doesn't mean anything," Sylvia said. "I've pretended to be sad for all sorts of dead people. And usually it was me that caused them to be that way."

A ripple of vampire humor went around the room. William and Olivia and I did not take part in the hilarity.

"From what you've described," Alfred spoke up from a far

couch, where he was busily knitting a colorful pair of socks. "My money's on William's financial planner." Then he turned to William. "Sorry, old chap. I've got a good man myself, if you're in the market for a new advisor."

I felt like we had a couple of steps to go through before we worried about finding William a new financial planner. Chief among them, proving that his current one had committed murder.

"We should get inside Jemima Taft's office. Discover what it is that was so vitally important that Felicity might blackmail her for it," Dr. Christopher Weaver said, not even pausing in his complicated stitchwork.

Sylvia nodded. "Perhaps Lucy should pose as a prospective client. Theodore could drive her up in the Bentley; he's a very good chauffeur. He plays that role frequently. In fact, it was he who drove us here tonight."

She glanced at me, in my usual attire of jeans and a hand-made sweater. This time one that Silence had made me. I didn't wear it very often because she had knit lace all around the collar and cuffs. The work was amazing and intricate and the stitches so tiny they looked like actual lace, but I felt like a Victorian maiden when I wore it. Besides, it was a little tight around the neck, and the way we kept talking about poor Felicity being strangled and garroted, the last thing I wanted was anything around my throat.

Sylvia continued, "We'd have to get you dressed well enough that she'd believe you had money, of course. Your grandmother and I could take you shopping to the designer boutiques." And then a wicked gleam came into her eye. "And I'd lend you some of my jewelry, but we all know how that turned out last time."

We all burst out laughing, even the mortals this time. If there was anything that was going to break the ice between me and

Sylvia, it was her joking about the last time she'd lent me her jewels.

When the laughter died down, I said, "I appreciate it, but I think she's already got a pretty good idea of my financial situation. She's seen my shop and"—I put my hands up—"the way I dress, the way I live."

Sylvia made a rude noise. "That doesn't mean anything. Look at the way William acts and dresses. Even worse, Olivia over there with the dirt ground into her hands. There are more rich people you'd pass in the street, my dear, than there are blowhard billionaires, believe me."

I did believe her.

"If Felicity was blackmailing Jemima, we must discover what she had on her friend," Gran suggested.

"Could it be something to do with this top-secret deal she's putting together?" Quickly I outlined as much as I could remember of the Hurst and Havers takeover.

There was a moment of stunned silence.

"Hurst and Havers? Are you certain, Lucy?" This news had made all of them stop knitting, so it must be big.

CHAPTER 24

"*Y*es. I'm sure. What's the big deal? It's a tailor, right?"

"It's a tailor the way the Hope Diamond is a chunk of coal," Alfred said. "Hurst and Havers have created my formal wear for nearly two hundred years. It's a British tradition. I thought its finances were solid."

"I guess not."

"But any number of decent companies would love to bid for it. That's why this deal is so secret," Alfred said, nodding.

I was glad he understood. I'd had to really work to dredge up the details of the secret deal, first, because I hadn't been that interested, and second, because there was a lot of champagne under the bridge by the time Jemima let the secret slip out.

Theodore said, "Essentially, it sounds like Jemima is the front person putting together a big-money deal with partners who don't necessarily know each other."

They all nodded. He looked at my puzzled face. "We do it all the time in our world. We find a mortal to be the coordinator, and we may not even know the other parties."

"It sounds like some shady, illegal drug cartel."

"It's not," Rafe said thoughtfully. "Very rich people who shun the spotlight, as we do, rarely want their business dealings to be public. In this case, privacy is crucial because the minute word gets out that Hurst and Havers is for sale, the price will go sky-high. Even I hadn't heard a whisper of their financial troubles." He looked quite irked that he hadn't.

"Jemima was horrified when she realized she'd been speaking out of turn while in her cups, especially in the Wainwright Hotel, where she was surrounded by wealthy, well-connected people." I cast my mind back to our walk. "She didn't know she'd talked. When I told her, she was stunned."

"If she's experiencing alcohol-induced amnesia, then she's got a problem," Theodore said.

I looked around at the vampires, all working away. I was glad Clara was working on my rug because I couldn't concentrate on murder and knit at the same time. "She's as cool as a cucumber in her professional dealings. Completely trustworthy and confidential. Right, William?"

"Oh, yes. The soul of discretion."

"Goes for dinner with her clients and doesn't even sip wine. And then in the evening, she gets together with her best friend who lets her rip. She was tipsy when I bumped into her and Felicity at the pub and flat-out drunk last night. I bet that's not the first time she's said things and didn't even remember she'd said them."

"A definite liability to the kind of people she works with."

William said, "I think I will look for a new financial advisor if that's the way she behaves."

That line of Rafe's about most murders being solved within twenty-four hours had somehow stuck with me. I felt the clock ticking. Felicity had been killed around three in the morning. It was nearly ten now. That left us five hours. I knew it was an arbitrary deadline, but I felt spurred on by that ticking clock. Panicky, like time was running out.

And then it hit me. No wonder I thought time was running out. It actually was.

I stood up. "I know who it is," I said. "And there's no time to lose."

I'D ALWAYS FOUND it pretty difficult to surprise vampires. They'd seen and done it all. However, my statement did raise some eyebrows.

"But who is it? How can you possibly know?" Alfred wanted to know.

"No time. I'll explain later. William? Do you know where Jemima's office is?"

"Yes. It's difficult to find, though. There's no plate outside."

"We need to go there right now. Before it's too late."

I was already up and grabbing my bag.

"But—"

"Get in the car, and I'll tell you on the way."

Naturally, every member of the vampire knitting club jumped to their feet, as did Olivia and William.

"I can't take all of you. William, you'll have to come." There was no question of Rafe coming along. He was already by my side. Sylvia's penetrating, theatrical voice rang out.

"Theodore, drive them in the Bentley. Don't argue. He's an excellent driver. And a good man in a pinch."

None of us could argue with that.

I knew that Rafe wanted to take his own car, but he must see, as I did, that this way we'd be free to jump out without having to worry about finding parking, which was always a nightmare in Oxford.

We ran out into the night and piled into the Bentley.

The road leading from Crosyer Manor back into Oxford is

generally a peaceful, scenic drive. It's one lane either way with trees that meet overhead, really pretty in certain lights when the sun peeks through and makes lace of shadows on the road. There are thickets of trees, the remains of Wychwood Forest, and rolling fields with stone cottages and farms to look at. But at night, when you're in a screaming hurry down a winding road with no streetlights, trying to save somebody's life, let's just say it's not the Autobahn.

"Call Jemima. Tell her you need to see her urgently about business."

"What business? I barely look at my monthly statements. I leave all that to her."

"I don't know." I didn't have any investment statements to worry me.

"You think you've found a discrepancy in the accounting," Rafe suggested. "That will get her attention."

Oh, good one.

William had his mobile phone out and was trying to call Jemima. Naturally, Jemima Taft wasn't picking up. He left a message. Several messages as he kept calling. Then, on the fourth, he just said, "Call me. It's urgent."

"It was Jemima who was the intended victim," I said, finally seeing the truth. "Not Felicity. Everybody remarked on how similar they were. Similar size and build, similar hairstyle, a little bit similar in looks. But the killer didn't know that Felicity had gone to stay at Jemima Taft's house."

"But there were two of them in the house," Theodore reminded me. "Why not kill both women?"

"The guest room is on the main floor. But Jemima's bedroom is on the top floor. He must have gone inside the room in the dark, seen a woman who looked like Jemima, killed her and left. Job done."

"But why?" William asked. "If it was Jemima who was the

target, what was the reason?" He stiffened. "She isn't really stealing clients' money, is she?"

"No. She's an excellent financial advisor but for one fatal flaw. She drinks, and then she talks."

"She was spilling secrets," Rafe said, nodding.

"Exactly. The killer needed to stop Jemima blabbing the most delicate, confidential secrets all over Oxford every time she got drunk."

"But how did the killer know she was doing it? You said yourself she was the epitome of discretion all day long in her business dealings."

"Because he overheard her," I said. Suddenly I saw the scene playing out in my head. How had I been so stupid I hadn't seen this before?

To William, I said, "He was even at your dinner party. Remember how she said that was such an important dinner party? And she and Nico were both fussing over the menu? She brought together people who, between them, could buy the struggling business and could afford to turn it around, thus making yet another fortune."

"But how did Felicity end up being at the dinner? Perhaps you've wronged her, Lucy, and she had the high net worth required of Felicity's clients."

"No. She was a last-minute addition. The only other woman couldn't make it. Rather than re-order the table, she invited Felicity, who was desperate to marry rich."

"That makes sense."

"Are you saying that Nico is our killer?"

"It had to be someone at that dinner, but I'm pretty sure it's him."

Theodore looked rather pleased with himself. "I was waiting until later, but I did do a little digging on everyone who was at your dinner. I think Lucy's right. All of them seem perfectly legitimate on the surface, but when you dig, it's like you tunnel down and find yourself popping up back at the surface again. That always makes me suspicious."

I smiled, because for all his cherubic looks, Theodore was suspicious of everything and everybody.

He followed William's directions, although I suspected Theodore already knew where we were going. He wouldn't have been much of a private investigator if he hadn't already checked out Jemima's place of business. Her investment firm was located in the upper floor of an elegant stone building on Broad Street. The street level contained a gift shop, but according to William, the investment firm offices took up the second and third floors.

"The lights are on upstairs. That has to be good," I said as Theodore pulled up.

I pointed to where a black Mercedes sat idling right in front of the building's door. "And that's her car and driver. That has to be a good sign. She hasn't left yet. And I'm guessing she's alive because she always texts him when she's ready to go and then he appears like magic in front of her door."

"That's a relief," Rafe said. "We've a chance to catch our killer then. Presumably he'll follow her home if he plans to do away with her tonight."

"Yes. They were probably waiting until she'd finished the deal. Sign the contracts, get the deal in motion, and then Jemima's no longer an asset. She's a liability."

At that moment, the door opened and Jemima came out. She was laughing, looking very pleased with herself. Beside her was Nico. And something about the expression on his face as he looked at her made my blood run cold. I was probably being fanciful, but he had the same look a hawk has when it's about to swoop down on innocent prey.

He walked her to the car and opened the back door himself.

She slid into the back of the Mercedes, and to my shock and horror, Nico slid in after her.

"Oh, that's not good," I said.

"He won't attempt to kill her, not in the car, with her driver right there," Theodore said.

But I think we all felt the tension in the air. And then, just as we were about to pull out and follow the car, Rafe said, "That's not her driver."

I followed his gaze and saw her driver, her real driver, Dick, come staggering from a nearby doorway. Blood was trickling down his face. He tried to call out and then crumpled.

"William, go and stay with him. See if there's anything you can do. Call the ambulance and the police," Rafe instructed.

William jumped out and ran to the man lying crumpled on the ground.

I wanted to help, too, but I suspected Jemima Taft needed our help more.

CHAPTER 25

J wanted Theodore to jam his foot on the gas and tear after the car containing Jemima and her potential killer, but Theodore eased into the sparse traffic, leaving a fair distance between the Mercedes and us. I knew intellectually he was doing the right thing, not alerting them to our presence. The Bentley wasn't exactly a stealth vehicle. He was doing his best to remain out of the killer's sight.

"It must be one of his men driving. They're taking no chances," Rafe said.

Theodore agreed, "They're not going to take her back to her house. He's heading out of town. I imagine they're going to kill her and ditch her body. Make it look like an accident." Theodore seemed to ponder alternatives. "Perhaps they'll make it look as though she took her own life. No doubt they'll leave abundant evidence that she killed her friend and was filled with remorse."

He wove around a van. "Good thing we arrived when we did or I rather think they'd have come back to finish off her driver."

I was getting panicky now. Had Jemima figured out something was wrong? They weren't going in the right direction for her house. Or was charming Nico stringing her along with some surprise he had in mind? I hoped he was. I didn't want to think of her terrified, not knowing that we were right behind her.

"Can't you overtake them or something?" I asked.

"Patience, Lucy," Theodore said. I would never forget how he remained calm while I was so nervous and stressed, I couldn't sit still. Even Rafe, normally completely unflappable, sat straighter than usual. He reached out and gripped my hand, which helped.

I said, "Can't you do some like vampire super-speed thing and catch them?"

"It hasn't come to that yet," Theodore said, sounding for all the world like we were on a Sunday drive. "Be patient."

Patience was about the last thing I had in stock right now. I tried to think of some spell that would stop a speeding car, but I didn't have one. I now knew how to put a hex on someone, but if I put a hex on Nico, it wouldn't kick in until tomorrow. That would be far too late.

While I was having these thoughts, the car was on the ring road out of Oxford. Rafe and Theodore spoke in low tones that I couldn't hear. Which was very annoying. They turned off onto one of the smaller byways leading out of town, and Rafe said, "Good. Hold on, Lucy. You've got your seat belt on tight?"

Was this really the time for a seat belt check? But I nodded. I was well strapped in.

We were on a B road, with sparse traffic, and I could see Rafe scanning ahead out the window. His night vision was, of course, superhuman, so where I saw darkness with smudges of light from houses, he probably saw every detail clearly.

After a few knuckle-biting minutes, as we cruised along the road, the Mercedes nothing but a pair of taillights some ways in front, Rafe said, "Now."

Theodore sped up behind the car in front and then pulled out as though he were going to pass. Again, we were on a road that was one lane each way. We were now in the path of oncoming traffic. Fortunately, there wasn't any, but I was starting to be as concerned about my safety as I was about Jemima's.

Instead of pulling to the side, the Mercedes sped up. Theodore drove even faster. They must have done something to the Bentley's engine. This stately old dreamboat could final at Daytona.

And then to my absolute shock because I hadn't been expecting it, Theodore suddenly turned the wheel hard, and the Bentley rammed the other vehicle.

The Bentley is a magnificent car. It's heavy and solid, and when it's made up its mind on a course of action, it's very stubborn. There was a horrible sound of metal grinding on metal, sparks flew, and the Mercedes nearly went off the road.

I could see the driver. He looked like a thug, but to give him credit, he was an excellent driver. He managed to hang on to the wheel and get back on the road.

Theodore went at him again.

There was another sickening impact. This time the car went right off the road. The countryside of Oxfordshire isn't full of cliffs. There was no dramatic dive. The car went into a ditch, out the other side, hit a tree and stalled.

The Bentley was still rolling to a stop when Rafe jumped out. There was a blur of motion, and suddenly he had the back of the town car open. With one arm, he yanked a terrified Jemima out.

She was shaking and crying. Also babbling, but he just brought her over and opened the door of the Bentley and pushed her in beside me.

Her eyes opened wide. "Lucy? What on earth are you doing here?"

"You're safe now," I told her, watching as Theodore joined Rafe. I admit I half expected them to go with the sharp-toothed brand of justice, but instead they used their superhuman strength and within no time had those plastic zip-tie handcuff things restraining two very angry Italians.

Theodore came back and opened the rear door. "Are you all right, ladies?" he asked, looking concerned.

"Yes," I answered. Jemima just nodded. She was in shock, shaking and sniffling.

Rafe said, "Theodore, call the police and stay with the culprits. I'll send someone back to fetch you."

"It will be my pleasure," Theodore said, looking delighted. Since he had a private investigator's license, he was always more than pleased to help the police in their endeavors. Especially if he got one over on them.

Rafe took the wheel of the Bentley, and we headed much more sedately back to town. Jemima put her head into her hands. "How did you know where I was, Lucy? They were going to kill me."

"Yes. I know," I said, handing her a tissue from my bag.

"You saved my life. You and your friend."

"Do you know why?" I had to ask. I had my theory about Felicity's murder and her near miss, but I wanted to hear her story.

"I've been such a fool," she said. "I trusted Nico. We put together a tremendous, most lucrative deal. He said we were going out to celebrate. I asked him to take me home so I could change, and then I noticed we weren't headed for my house. I told my driver he was going the wrong way, but it wasn't my driver."

"No."

"They were going to kill me," she said again, her voice shrill. "Nico said I couldn't be trusted. Said I had loose lips. I, who value discretion above all."

"You're going to have to tell the police everything, you know."

"I suppose I'll have to. Though it goes against the habits of a lifetime to break confidence with my clients."

"But you did break it. When you were inebriated last night, you started talking about this deal. You told us everything."

She put her head in her hands. "I'm so ashamed. I know I drink too much, but I've always thought I deserved to let my hair down when I work so hard all day. Anyway, even though I was obviously saying things I shouldn't, it was only you and Felicity. How did Nico hear about it? Unless Felicity was really secretly working for him."

I shook my head. I'd been wondering the same thing. "Was it his idea to have dinner at the Wainwright?"

"Yes. It was. But it's one of the best restaurants in Oxford. There was nothing wrong with that."

"Except that I think he was staying there too. When I went to find the bathroom, he walked by. He must have overheard you." I thought again about that waiter who was always hovering, ready to fill our champagne. "Maybe he even bribed the waiter after we left to find out what we'd been talking about."

"I've been such a fool," she said again.

I didn't think she was going to become less foolish if she kept repeating that more times.

"And now Felicity's dead." She turned to gaze at me. "Did Nico kill Felicity?"

"I believe so. Or somebody who worked for him. My guess is they thought she was you."

I went through my theory again about Felicity sleeping on the main floor and Jemima being tucked in on a higher floor.

"Poor Felicity. She always did want to be me, and she finally got her wish."

CHAPTER 26

"*I* don't know what to do or where to go," Jemima said, sounding half hysterical.

"That's easy," Rafe said. "We're taking you straight to the police."

"But I haven't done anything wrong."

"No. They'll want a full statement from you. You are the one who can tie your friend Nico to Felicity's murder."

I added, "And your attempted murder. Had he made it clear that was his plan tonight?"

"Not in so many words. He said he had a surprise for me. I admit I grew quite frightened. I asked him to take me straight home, but he only laughed. He said I talked too much and had to be taught a lesson."

I suppose, from a policing standpoint, it would have been better if Nico had had a length of clothesline in his hands and was wrapping some around Jemima's throat when he was pushed off the road. However, I suspected that there would be enough evidence that the police could put together a solid case.

And at least Jemima was still alive.

After we dropped Jemima off at the police station, we

headed back to Crosyer Manor. Naturally, the remaining vampires were still knitting away, clearly waiting to hear the outcome of the evening's adventures.

I had dreaded telling Sylvia about the Bentley, but Rafe took charge. "We apprehended the murderer," he said. "Theodore was brilliant. He's stayed to turn the killers over to the police."

"And Jemima?" Olivia wanted to know.

"She's safe. William stayed behind to help her driver, who was attacked." While everyone was on a high from that news, he said, "I'm sorry, Sylvia. The Bentley sustained some damage."

For a second, her eyes flashed, as they tended to do when she wasn't best pleased, but then she shrugged. "I know a good mechanic. And if it's completely ruined, I suppose I'll have to buy a new one. Perhaps a different color would be nice."

I could imagine Sylvia buying a different Bentley to match every outfit.

After we'd talked through the whole evening's adventures and everyone congratulated everyone else on a job well done, Hester said, "Now can I show you my coat? I worked all day to get it finished so I could show it off this evening."

My grandmother stood up and began to put her knitting away. "No, Hester. Not this evening. Olivia and Lucy have had a very big day. We have to remember they're only mortal. They need their sleep. You can show us your coat on Thursday."

"But—" her whine was cut off before it had properly started when Alfred took her arm and pulled her to her feet.

"Come on. I've got a tricky computer problem at home that needs sorting out. I was hoping you could help me. No one understands computers the way you do."

She was too egotistical not to fall for his ruse, and so she allowed herself to be led out. The rest of the vampires, taking the hint, quickly left, Alfred offering to drive the Bentley and pick up Theodore who, having handed Nico over to the police, found himself in need of a ride.

When they'd gone, Olivia said, "I'll call William. No doubt he'll need a ride home, too."

"Thank you, Olivia."

"I feel dreadful about poor Felicity, but at least now we know who killed her and why. I'll sleep a little easier. I know William will, too."

She left the room without even asking if Rafe needed anything else for the night. Such uncharacteristic Thresher behavior that I knew the events of the past couple of days had really gotten to her. After she left, I settled on the couch where I'd sat earlier. Nyx was curled up sound asleep on my herringbone rug, which Clara had left almost halfway completed. I'd have to remember to thank her in the morning.

"Will William be okay?" I asked Rafe, who didn't sit beside me, as I assumed he would. He couldn't seem to settle.

"Yes. A change of scene might do him good."

I raised my eyebrows. "A change of scene?"

He walked toward the long windows and gazed out into the back garden. "Lucy," he said, his face averted.

A niggle of dread began to poke at me as I looked at him standing there so still.

He said, "I'm going away."

The niggle turned into a full-on tsunami of dread. "Going away?" My voice came out too high. I pulled myself together and tried again. "Where are you going?"

"New Zealand."

"New Zealand? Why are you going there?"

"That curious book I was showing you, that I bought from a New Zealand collector. She's got several volumes that she'd like me to look at. They're kept in a properly controlled environment, too precious to travel. I must go to them."

"And you're going to take William with you?" I thought about it and nodded. "That's probably the best thing for him. A couple of weeks away will take his mind off Felicity. He could try out New Zealand restaurants and walk along the beach and whatever else you do in New Zealand." I'd never been there, so I was making this up as I went along.

Rafe turned to me at last, and his eyes looked as wintry as I'd ever seen them. "Not a couple of weeks, Lucy. We'll be gone indefinitely."

"No." The word was out before I could stop it.

He smiled, a slow, sad smile. "I can't do this anymore, you see. I can't see you, want you, fight my constant desire to have you with me. Part of me. It's too painful."

My heart was beating hard. "I know I haven't given you an answer, and I should have. I'm so sorry. It's just—"

He stopped me with a raised hand. "You don't need to explain. I understand the situation perfectly. I think, perhaps, in your situation, no decision is still a decision."

I sat there, staring. My heart felt like it had forgotten how to beat.

"I don't want you to go."

He looked so sad. "I have to."

It was my fault. I'd been so wretchedly indecisive. I tried to tell him how I felt. "It's not that I don't love you," I began.

"I know. You don't have to explain. I understand. And I want you to know, wherever you are, if you ever need me, I'll be there for you."

I could feel tears pooling in my eyes. "Will I ever see you again?"

There was a pause. "Yes. I'm sure you will, but I don't know when."

I felt like I couldn't breathe. There wasn't enough air in the room. After a moment, he said, "I'm going to my office now to prepare what I need to take with me."

This had to be the most awkward goodbye ever. I got to my feet and went towards him. "When are you leaving?"

"Tomorrow."

"So soon?"

He didn't say anything, just opened his arms, and I went into them. We held each other for a long time. He kissed me, gently and sweetly, then without another word, he walked out of the room.

CHAPTER 27

The next morning at Cardinal Woolsey's, Violet and I were two of the least engaging salespeople in the history of retail.

Her eyes were red and swollen from crying. So were mine. I had expected that I would have to be the one to deliver the news to her that William was leaving for an indefinite period of time, but he'd phoned her himself. He'd also filled her in on the whole story of Jemima Taft and the real reason Felicity Stevens had been murdered.

Normally we would have talked it through and exclaimed over all the high points of the murder investigation, but today, neither of us could be bothered.

"We might as well just put up the closed sign," I said. "I can't make the effort to sell wool."

"I know what you mean." She sighed. "Shall I put the kettle on?"

"Why not?"

Everything seemed pointless today. Even Nyx looked depressed. Her little head hung out of her basket, and she followed me with big, sad eyes as though it was all my fault.

Which I supposed it was. Rafe wouldn't be leaving if it wasn't for me, and if he wasn't leaving, he wouldn't be taking William with him, thus depriving Violet of yet another romantic possibility.

We drank tea and moped some more.

When I couldn't stand my own misery any longer, I said, "Can you hold the fort? I'm going to visit my grandmother for a while."

Violet didn't look very pleased that I was leaving her alone, but it wasn't like we were run off our feet with customers. "Don't be too long," she said, as though she were my boss.

I headed downstairs into the tunnels and made my way to the vampires' lair. I knocked softly in case they were all sleeping, which they often were at this time of day, but Sylvia opened the door right away. I didn't want to talk to her. I was in no mood.

"Is my grandmother here?"

She looked slightly taken aback at my abruptness, but she nodded. "Come in."

Sure enough, Gran was sitting in the corner of one of the opulent settees, knitting away. Sylvia's knitting was on the couch opposite her. There was no one else in the room. With an unusual display of tact, Sylvia picked up her knitting and disappeared into her own rooms. Gran looked at me.

"What is it, Lucy?"

This was why I'd come here. Gran was always the person I'd gone to when my heart had been broken or I had a problem I couldn't solve. I threw myself into her arms.

"I don't know what to do," I wailed.

She patted my back and simply waited. After a minute, I poured out all my feelings, how conflicted I was about Rafe, how I didn't want him to leave but how much I understood that he needed to go. I was getting into such a mess, our conversation was like one of my knitting projects. Nothing but tangles and false starts and holes.

She didn't say anything, just let me talk it through.

She looked as sad as I felt when I told her he was leaving and I didn't think I'd be seeing much more of him in the future. "You can't blame him, Lucy. He loves you."

"And I love him." As I said the words, I felt how true they were. "But there are some pretty big issues between us."

Suddenly the line that I still thought Nyx had put in my head popped back again. "Love is always the answer."

Gran thought for a minute and then said, "Without Rafe confusing you, you'll meet a perfectly nice mortal man. You'll have children. You'll age together. You'll struggle and argue and do all the things people normally do."

I looked at her. "But I'll never be normal, will I?"

She shook her head. "You're a witch. You'll never not be a witch."

I sighed and sank back into the couch. "I was doomed before I began. I can't live a normal life."

"But you could live a mortal one," she reminded me. "And I've heard from Hester there's a special dating site for witches. What was it called? Witch Date?"

I shook my head vehemently. "Anything but that."

"You mustn't worry, dear. Give it time. Rafe will fade from your thoughts, and someone new will take his place."

And yet, the more she said those supposedly comforting words, the more I grew panicked. I didn't want some normal man. It wouldn't be his fault, but he'd bore me to tears. He'd never be able to compare to Rafe Crosyer, who understood me in a way no mortal man ever could. Who was always there when I needed him. Who loved me enough to accept that I would age and die. Who loved me enough to want to marry me anyway.

I'd been so busy thinking about the conflicts between us that I'd stopped myself from thinking about all the positive aspects of our relationship. I loved his intelligence and his wide knowledge of the world, of history, art, books and all the things that I wanted to understand and didn't. He was gorgeous and sexy and had a sly wit about him. I'd become fond of William and Olivia and even Henri the peacock. And not only me; what about Nyx? She'd be brokenhearted not to have Rafe in her life anymore.

I jumped up suddenly. I felt this terrible sense of urgency. "Gran, I've got to go."

She didn't look very surprised. In fact, her eyes twinkled as though she'd known all along the decision I'd end up making.

"You think he's right for me, don't you?"

She looked at me with her wise, old eyes. "It's not for me to decide your future. All I can say is, there's a great deal that's right about you two together. Love is rarely convenient, my dear. Never perfect. But when you find it, grab it with both hands."

"But he'll outlive me. I don't want him to be sad."

"Wouldn't you take a few years of perfect happiness, even if you knew you'd then have to live without it?"

I nodded slowly. "Yes." Panic was beating away inside me. "What if I'm too late? What if he's gone?"

"Don't waste time asking me pointless questions. Get in your car and go to him."

"Right. Right." Then I hugged her. "Thanks, Gran."

I ran upstairs and said to Violet, "I won't be back for the rest of the day. If you need help, call my grandmother. She'll send Clara and Mabel up to help in the shop."

"Whoa. Where are you going?"

"I'm going to fix the dumbest mistake I ever almost made. And I don't have time to explain."

She must have known what I was referring to, for she brightened up immediately. "Don't worry. Leave the shop in my capable hands."

Even in all my rush, I had time to sprint back and give her a quick hug. "Wish me luck."

"You know I do."

I wanted to put on something pretty and do my makeup, but there was no time. I grabbed my cell phone and called William. He answered right away, sounding sad.

"I'm so glad you called, Lucy. Sorry I didn't get a chance to say goodbye to you properly."

"Never mind that. Where are you? What time are you leaving?"

"We're nearly packed. We should be gone within minutes."

"No. You can't leave."

"Lucy. My time's not my own. Rafe is like a man possessed."

"You don't want to go to New Zealand, do you?"

"Well, not permanently."

"I think if I can just talk to Rafe, I might be able to talk him out of this crazy trip. Do whatever you have to. I don't know, pull the distributor cap out of the Range Rover. Pull the battery out of the Tesla." This was the extent of my car-mechanics knowledge. Obviously, nobody would ever confuse me with a grease monkey.

He began to chuckle. "You're a crazy woman, do you know that?"

"I'm beginning to realize it." By this time I was in my car, a birthday present that Rafe had organized. So many of the nice things he'd done for me were gathering together like a bouquet of flowers in my imagination. I'd nearly let all this go.

I drove as fast as I could, which wasn't really all that fast, as I was still scared of the left-hand side of the road thing. When I finally got to the drive into Crosyer Manor, my heart was banging hard from the fear I'd be too late.

But to my eternal relief, Rafe was standing looking anything but pleased while William had the hood pulled up on the Range Rover and appeared to be poking at its innards.

I was so happy to see them, I nearly cried. I pulled up behind the vampire.

Rafe turned, and first his eyes lit with joy, and then I could see the pain descend on them. I got out of the car, and his face was set. Impassive.

"Lucy. What are you doing here?" Not said in a very welcoming tone.

"Is there somewhere we could talk? In private?"

He glanced at his watch like a busy man with places he really had to be. "I suppose so." And irritably he said to William, "And you'd better call a mechanic."

William sent me the ghost of a wink and said, "Will do."

Rafe marched ahead of me to the door of the manor house and unlocked it. It was so weird to see him use a key. Always in the past, somebody had been inside ready to open it as part of his smoothly oiled lifestyle. Now we walked into a house that was already feeling like it was empty. Even though I knew that Olivia was still on the grounds, she didn't live in the house. Without Rafe and William here, no one would.

He walked ahead of me into the drawing room and then turned. Behind him, the wintry light made the trees look like so many skeletons.

"What is it?"

Oh, he was not making this easy for me. I don't know what I'd expected. That he'd open his arms when he saw me? I could see that he'd made his decision and he was on his way.

I had so many things rolling around in my head, I couldn't find the right thing to say, so I just said, "Yes."

He looked irritable. "Yes, what?"

I could hardly get the words out now. My throat was getting choked up. "The answer to your question. The answer is yes. I'll marry you."

Again, he acted completely opposite to what any normal

man in love with a woman might do, live or undead. His face closed down even more.

"No."

I felt like he'd hit me. I sat down on the couch because my legs wouldn't hold me up anymore. "No? Don't you love me after all?"

"Lucy, I love you far too much to accept anything but the same in return. Don't say yes in order to keep me here."

I saw now how much I'd hurt him with my indecision. I stood up and went to him and took his hands in mine. I looked up, right into his eyes, and let him see everything I was feeling. "You were right. It was the thought of losing you that made my decision so clear. But I'm not saying yes for any other reason than that I don't want to live my life without you. I want us to be together and live whatever crazy life we have in front of us for as long as we have it. I'm yours."

For a moment, I watched the war going on behind his eyes. It was like the bleak, gray sky outside, and then I saw the moment the sun broke through.

"You're sure about this?"

"Never surer of anything."

He kissed me as though he'd never let me go. And then he said, "Wait here a minute."

I assumed he was going to tell William he could stop messing around with the car. Who knew what the man had done to it? But instead, Rafe ran upstairs in the direction of the bedrooms. What on earth?

He was back in no time holding a jewelry box.

I began to tremble as he got down on one knee. "Lucy Swift, will you make me the happiest creature on earth? Will you marry me?"

My voice was husky as I said, "Yes."

He opened the ring box, and I cried out with delight. With his wealth, I'd have expected he might give me some overpriced, pretentious bauble, but I should have known better. This ring was perfect. A square cut emerald flanked by diamonds. I remembered looking in jewelry store windows with my grandmother back when she'd been alive, and how impressed I'd been that she knew the meanings of various stones. I'd fallen for a ring very much like this one. I could almost hear her voice. "Emerald is for the heart Chakra. And diamonds are about stepping into your power."

"Also eternal love," my eternal love reminded me.

I slipped it on my finger, and naturally, the ring fit perfectly. Rafe was normally so sure of himself that it was wonderful to see him look uncertain.

"Do you really like it?"

I held it away so I could admire the fire in the depths of the diamond. "I can't even tell you. It's exactly what I would have chosen for myself."

"Good. Your grandmother helped me pick it out."

Now my eyes opened wide. "Seriously?"

"She did. I had a few ideas in mind, and she steered me in the right direction."

I began to laugh. I recalled that speech Gran had given me about choosing a mortal man, when all the time she'd obviously been hoping I'd choose Rafe.

"You should tell William. And get him to put your car back together again."

"What are you—"

"I called him. I told him to do whatever he had to do to keep you here until I arrived."

He began to laugh then. "I'm going to have to keep my eye on you."

In the end, we went out together to tell William the good

news. He looked delighted, and I didn't think it was only because he didn't want to go to New Zealand. He hugged me.

"Lucy, this is a great day for all of us. I look forward to serving you as I do Rafe."

I was about to tell him no, no, we were friends, but I realized how important it was to be Rafe's partner in all things, even if it meant accepting I now had household staff. So all I said was, "Thank you."

Naturally, Olivia had to be told. And she was as thrilled as William had been. She put her arm around him. "This means I won't lose my big brother."

"Not quite yet."

William turned to Rafe. "I'll phone the airport and tell the pilot to stand down."

Of course Rafe had his own plane. Had I really thought he'd be traveling on British Airways?

He shook his head. "No. Tell them we're on our way." We all stared at him.

"You're still going?" That was me. William and Olivia were much less likely to question their boss.

He turned to me and grabbed my hands. His eyes were alight with excitement. "I've been wanting to show you all my favorite places. I do need to go to New Zealand. Come with me. Then we can go anywhere you want. I have a world of places I want to share with you. We can stop in Egypt if you like so you can tell your parents the news in person."

He'd thought of everything. I was stunned. "But the shop."

"Violet can run it in your absence. And you know several vampires who would be only too happy to help."

I flapped my arms around. "I don't have any clothes. I don't even have a toothbrush."

"Details. We'll stop in Paris on the way and do some shopping."

Oh, we'd stop in Paris on the way and do some shopping. Of course we would.

"There's Nyx and Gran."

"Call your grandmother on the way. She'll look after Nyx. They'll be good company for each other."

"How long will you be gone?" William asked him.

"Three weeks or thereabouts. Does that give you time to plan the wedding?"

William grinned at him. "Weddings are my specialty."

He looked at me again. "Well?"

He was so outrageous, it was impossible. And yet, suddenly everything seemed possible. "Fine. But don't think when we're married you can boss me around like this, because you can't."

He took my hand and kissed it. "I'll remember that."

Thank you so much for reading *Herringbones and Hexes*. Want to know what happens next? Check out *Ribbing and Runes*.

RIBBING AND RUNES

© 2021 NANCY WARREN

CHAPTER 1

Planning a wedding is stressful at the best of times, but when the groom is a vampire who's been around for more than half a millennium, the guest list gets complicated. However, Rafe and I had easily agreed that we wanted to keep the number of guests to a reasonable limit.

The vampire knitting club were all invited. I'd asked my cousin Violet to be a bridesmaid, and our friend Alice had agreed to be the matron of honor. William Thresher would stand up for Rafe and he'd asked an old friend from Ireland, Lochlan Balfour, to be his only groomsman.

So far, so good. Then came my trickiest dilemma.

What was I going to do about Gran? She was a vampire, but too recently turned to appear in public. But how could I not invite my beloved grandmother to my wedding?

It was a dilemma I couldn't solve and Gran who came up with the solution. "My love," she said, "I can watch your wedding from the window."

The wedding would be held at Rafe's manor house and there

were so many rooms with windows in the estate that it would be simple to arrange the ceremony so Gran had a perfect view. I hugged her. "It won't be the same as having you right there, but it's a brilliant idea."

"I'll be right beside you in spirit, as you know," she replied.

Once we'd solved that problem, the organization proceeded surprisingly well. William was a brilliant caterer and event planner. Both Rafe and I wanted the wedding here in the home I'd soon share, so it all fell into place smoothly.

We didn't put an announcement in the local paper or anything as we wanted a private affair, but somehow word got out. To my delight, congratulations-on-your-engagement cards started arriving at the shop and Rafe's home, as well as a few gifts.

I was at Rafe's enjoying one of William's delicious dinners. He'd had some fresh Scottish salmon sent to him and prepared it simply, grilled with a heavenly sauce containing lemon and dill, rice pilaf and fresh asparagus. Rafe sat with me and we chatted about everything. Now that I'd accepted my feelings for him and his proposal, we were free to share all our thoughts and feelings, knowing we'd be part of each other's lives until death did us part. Mine, most likely, but I pushed that thought away.

When William returned to clear my all-but-licked-clean plate, he brought in a wrapped gift. "This came for you both by private courier."

"Ooh, a present," I squealed.

Rafe looked amused. "You're like a small child at Christmas."

"I don't care what you think. I love presents."

"Then you'd better open it."

I pulled the silver ribbon away and happily tore into the white and silver paper. Inside was a white cardboard box with the name of a shop written in gold script on the lid. I barely glanced at it as I removed the lid and peeked inside.

I saw something wooden that appeared old. Gingerly, I lifted out a box with strange symbols carved into it. I thought at first the writing was Egyptian hieroglyphics, which I can read having spent many a summer helping my archaeologist parents on digs. However, while the symbols were similar, they weren't Egyptian.

I showed Rafe who accepted the box and studied the inscription. "These are runes," he said. "Very old. I wonder if this is from Lochlan." He glanced around. "Was there a card?"

I'd been so eager to unwrap the present I hadn't even looked for a card. Now we searched, but there wasn't any indication who the gift had come from. "Open the box," I said. "Maybe there's a card inside."

Sometimes, I'm not so smart.

Order your copy today! *Ribbing and Runes* is Book 13 in the Vampire Knitting Club series.

A Note from Nancy

Dear Reader,

Thank you for reading the Vampire Knitting Club series. I am so grateful for all the enthusiasm this series has received. I have plenty more stories about Lucy and her undead knitters planned for the future.

I hope you'll consider leaving a review and please tell your friends who like cozy mysteries.

Review on Amazon, Goodreads or BookBub.

Your support is the wool that helps me knit up these yarns.

Join my newsletter for a free prequel, *Tangles and Treasons*, the exciting tale of how the gorgeous Rafe Crosyer was turned into a vampire.

I hope to see you in my private Facebook Group. It's a lot of fun. www.facebook.com/groups/NancyWarrenKnitwits

Until next time,
Happy Reading,

Nancy

ALSO BY NANCY WARREN

The best way to keep up with new releases, plus enjoy bonus content and prizes is to join Nancy's newsletter at nancywarrenuthor.com or join her in her private FaceBook group Nancy Warren's Knitwits.

~

The Great Witches Baking Show

The Great Witches Baking Show - Book 1

Baker's Coven - Book 2

A Rolling Scone - Book 3

A Bundt Instrument - Book 4

Blood, Sweat and Tiers - Book 5

Crumbs and Misdemeanors - Book 6

Gingerdead House - A Holiday Whodunnit

The Great Witches Baking Show Boxed Set: Books 1-3

Vampire Book Club

The Vampire Book Club - Book 1

Chapter and Curse - Book 2

A Spelling Mistake - Book 3

Vampire Knitting Club

Tangles and Treasons - a free prequel for Nancy's newsletter subscribers

The Vampire Knitting Club - Book 1

Stitches and Witches - Book 2

Crochet and Cauldrons - Book 3

Stockings and Spells - Book 4

Purls and Potions - Book 5

Fair Isle and Fortunes - Book 6

Lace and Lies - Book 7

Bobbles and Broomsticks - Book 8

Popcorn and Poltergeists - Book 9

Garters and Gargoyles - Book 10

Diamonds and Daggers - Book 11

Herringbones and Hexes - Book 12

Ribbing and Runes - Book 13

Cat's Paws and Curses - A Holiday Whodunnit

Vampire Knitting Club Boxed Set: Books 1-3

Vampire Knitting Club Boxed Set: Books 4-6

Toni Diamond Mysteries

Toni is a successful saleswoman for Lady Bianca Cosmetics in this
series of humorous cozy mysteries.

Frosted Shadow - Book 1

Ultimate Concealer - Book 2

Midnight Shimmer - Book 3

A Diamond Choker For Christmas - A Holiday Whodunnit

The Almost Wives Club

An enchanted wedding dress is a matchmaker in this series of romantic
comedies where five runaway brides find out who the best men
really are!

The Almost Wives Club: Kate - Book 1

Second Hand Bride - Book 2

Bridesmaid for Hire - Book 3

The Wedding Flight - Book 4

If the Dress Fits - Book 5

Take a Chance series

Meet the Chance family, a cobbled together family of eleven kids who are all grown up and finding their ways in life and love.

Kiss a Girl in the Rain - Book 1

Iris in Bloom - Book 2

Blueprint for a Kiss - Book 3

Every Rose - Book 4

Love to Go - Book 5

The Sheriff's Sweet Surrender - Book 6

The Daisy Game - Book 7

Chance Encounter - Prequel

Take a Chance Box Set - Prequel and Books 1-3

Abigail Dixon Mysteries

Death of a Flapper - Book 1

For a complete list of books, check out Nancy's website.

ABOUT THE AUTHOR

Nancy Warren is the USA Today Bestselling author of more than 70 novels. She's originally from Vancouver, Canada, though she tends to wander and has lived in England, Italy and California at various times. While living in Oxford she dreamed up The Vampire Knitting Club. Favorite moments include being the answer to a crossword puzzle clue in Canada's National Post newspaper, being featured on the front page of the New York Times when her book Speed Dating launched Harlequin's NASCAR series, and being nominated three times for Romance Writers of America's RITA award. She has an MA in Creative Writing from Bath Spa University. She's an avid hiker, loves chocolate and most of all, loves to hear from readers! The best way to stay in touch is to sign up for Nancy's newsletter at nancywarrenauthor.com or join her private Facebook group www.facebook.com/groups/NancyWarrenKnitwits

To learn more about Nancy and her books
nancywarrenauthor.com